Invistor Star
and
The Ja'Way   Water Spirit

Written by; R. W. Wright.

Who also wrote:-

'**The Invistor Star**' The original adventure, before the **Ja'Way water spirit**, and first in the series of three fictional romantic, action novels.

Gone & never said Goodbye ' A Nonfiction story of actuality.

About the author:
A well-travelled accomplished artist and musician. Born in Bexley, South London, England and brought up in Dehra-Dun near New Delhi Northern India. Then later, he moved to Brisbane, South Australia.
During the early part of his life, Ron lived in Libya for several years and then much later moved to Greece for twelve.
He has extensively travelled through Europe and the Mediterranean.

He is currently married and living in Cambridge England where he is engaged in two other fictional stories to be completed in 2017 / 2018.

THE INVISTOR STAR

And   the JAWAY or water spirit

ISBN 978-0-9573959-2-3
ISBN 9 780957 395923

Typeset in Times New Roman
Printed and bound in Great Britain by
Book Printing UK, Remus House, Peterborough

INVISTOR STAR
and
The JA'WAY or WATER SPIRIT

INTRODUCTION

The immortal words;
Some are born with Greatness and some have Greatness thrust upon them.
In this case, Captains Appisommati and Rocco Alexander Townsend, had no choice, it was to be thrust upon them, after their accidental discovery of the Crystal key, then ultimately the Star ship Ja'Way, or Water Spirit.
They had been walking in an area that had been undeveloped and covered in sand for centuries on a planet called Mayan.
The Ja'Way was historically known in the annuals of antiquity as the flag ship, the pride of the Mayan people and still a spoken legend with tales of invincibility.
 It had vanished centuries before when the area of discovery was still under the protection of the Sea. In the ancient journals of Mayan, the records showed a hand painted picture that had faded into a grey streak but, the name was described in part; by some broken, unreadable and faded Mayan characters, giving an air of mystery about its disappearance.
Its discovery now, after all this time, begs the question, that if Captain Rocco had not found the crystal key and the Invistor Star team had not detected the metallic object, would it ever have been found ? Of course the land movement and the natural erosion of the planet, would eventually release all its secrets. However, a long after all the local inhabitants, had departed this world.

~ 3 ~

The two Captains, as we have learnt in the previous story were brought together by unusual circumstances. They both now shared command of the battle cruiser Invistor Star, with futuristic and scientific technologies.

The return journey, of the Invistor Star, first from the present and then; after time travel, the past. Made it necessary, to divert from the normal route taken to their home planet of Moofee, in the Aelia Pulcheria Galaxy, thousands of light years away.

It was ultimately a joint decision, although Rocco had insisted that the change of direction would give them a wider experience of the Cosmos. Even though, he had never been further than his own home planet, Earth.

Rocco did not relay his fears. But, he had lost Appi once and could not bear the thought, of her death again.

He had learnt the hard way by returning in time to their original first meeting. He truly understood now; just how much he loved her.

On this second journey together, they had found a new planet that would qualify all their needs. They were exceedingly happy, with trusted and loyal friends on the planets of Mayan and Freedom.

They too, now had their ultimate desires of freedom, peace and love. But, greatest of all, the expected birth of their first child.

Chapters

CHAPTER ONE

Just one day before the launching celebrations, they had successfully collected a large quantity of crystals for Lord Tuwa's new star ship, The Ja'Way.
Surprisingly, the materials that this ship had been crafted with made it practically indestructible, no rust or corrosion and it only required minor servicing and tests. Rocco had made sure that all the shuttlecraft had also been serviced and that there were a number of spare Crystals for any emergency.
At last, they were ready for the first trial flight. The crew assembled with Captain Tuwa and his guest Rocco. They had invited their friend Sawston and Awotz from the planet Freedom, but Rocco had suggested it would be folly to not have some backup. They might need their help if anything went wrong during the test flight.
He had spoken privately to Sawston and his deputy and explained. ` You understand we are taking a great unknown risk. I trust in our friendship, that you will undertake to help the wives and families if anything goes wrong. ` He smiled. ` My friends, if we are successful we can start the initial stages of joining our two planets together. After that, you and Awotz will be given the opportunity to Captain your own craft. ` Sawston laughed nervously and replied, ` But Captain, we have nothing as big or as progressive. ` He was physically shaken when Rocco insisted by saying that; `You Will Soon!` The look of determination from the Captain was enough for Sawston to realise that this man would do everything that he had promised.

Meanwhile, Tuwa's enthusiasm as Captain and Lord Commander was only slightly exceeded by the new members of his volunteer crew. They had been well versed in the workings of Moofee space travel as Captains Appisommati and Rocco had spent a great deal of time giving as much information as they could. However, they could only relate to the Invistor Star, since the Ja`Way was in theory similar but as it proved to be; more advanced in technology. The crew appeared to be slowly realising and understanding what was expected of them. They may have been comforted by Rocco's remarks as he frequently shouted , ` It is far better to make as many mistakes as you can now and learn from them, than be second guessing at the speed of light. ` He had assumed that this craft could travel at light speed.

Tuwa had chosen a mixed crew with previous shuttlecraft experience in flying and engineering. He had also asked for an automaton, he actually wanted the one that had made the act of surrendered by walking outside on the shuttlecraft roof. This was the action that had brought them together in friendship.

The event, as is customary, did not go unrecorded and was the cause of some small irritation, between the two parties later, when Appi discovered that the records showed not only a great alliance and permanent peace, but also transcribed an astonishing statement of embellished events into the history journals of Mayan. These journals not only embarrassed the truth but also the integrity of the Moofee community, who received no credit, for their part in avoiding the inter-planetary war. However, the translation of the journal would not come to light, until much, much later in the future.

The Ja`Way, unlike the Invistor Star was not fitted with landing gear? Perhaps it had not been considered necessary if the community did live underwater as they now supposed.

These thoughts of uncertainty, had delayed the second attempt to launch. It was obvious that the Ja`Way had to be able to float on the sea and there was reluctance to test the theory and the ships buoyancy, which caused so much frustration, because of the crew's realisation that it could only be proved by a trial flight.

They did not want to delay any longer and agreed that they would make an attempt to raise the craft and dock in the sea as close to the shore as possible.

Rocco`s thoughts were on the ships shuttlecraft. `You know Tuwa; I believe that we are missing something on this ship. It`s such a vast vessel. There must be another way to exit! `

 How would one leave the ship with the tailgate closed? I mean, we would have to open it and if as you suggest we were on the sea next to the dock. ` We would all sink. ` They said in unison!!

Tuwa agreed, ` but we have no plans or working directions of any other device or way that would enable exodus, not even in an emergency. ` He paused. ` I would ask the computer guardian, Pakal. But, we have no ancient Mayan words for such things.

Rocco, tele-thought a message to his crew in the standby shuttle; they in turn transferred the communication on to Appi.

She was pleased to hear Rocco`s voice, ` I hope you will be back soon. ` Her voice was quiet and far away.  She had been taking a baby nap; on the Star and was surprised at his questions? ` As you know we do not use such a critical device but, I seemed to remember these words are some of the technical terms, that I have heard used, for description in conversation. They are designation, dissemination, and of course molecular transfer. ` She yawned. ` I waiting you. `

Rocco noted the words and joined Tuwa in the Command centre.

~ 8 ~

The voice of Pakal sounded; `By your command.` As Tuwa started. ` Pakal, what other exit is there from the Ja`Way. `
The voice started to explain about the rear entrance, where they had entered. But, Tuwa interrupted. 'There must be another emergency exit. Surely, the shuttlecraft would not be used just to exit this craft or to transfer personnel to another place or ship. `
Rocco asked about designation and dissemination with no results. Until, he said the words molecular transfer. This prompted Tuwa to search his mind for the Ancient Mayan words for ` Leaving Spirit` or `Scatter Person` in combination with other terms that, in those ancient days they might have used. Then, by swapping the words around; Pakal, suddenly picked up `Choc- Winik. ` An ancient term, that meant scatter a person in Mayan. Pakal explained. `
That this was a device, able to dematerialise and move any material object to another place or position.
The device is situated on a lower deck near the engineering area. Pakel's voice changed to a deeper tone of authority.
`WARNING, –WARNING! It is forbidden by Lord Tec-Noc this Device is flawed. ` Pakal continued. ` This device was found to be dangerous with the transfer of carbon based life forms. ` Tuwa looked at Rocco, 'does he mean crew members. ` Rocco nodded as Pakal continued. ` Lord Tec-Noc, Captain and previous master, banned and disassembled the Choc-Winik after closing it down. His loss was too great to bear after a close friend and other crew members died using the machine. `
`Well, well, ` Rocco`s face was serious now, ` after all this time searching, perhaps someone could help figure it out. Molecular transfer! I have heard of it, but never believed it could be possible. ` He then, as usual stated the obvious. ` This ship has everything that one would desire. Except, a way off!`

They had to accept the facts, build a landing gear around the ship or repair the device known as Choc-Winik   or transporter.

Abandoning the ship was out of the question. Rocco called attention to the dilemma and since a gathering was already made in Engineering, they should initiate trials and experiment with the known principles until they established a working manual.

He glanced, as he was speaking to the rear of the group, and noticed a new arrival accompanied by Appi.

` I have brought some help, ` she smiled` My Engineering Android may be familiar with some of the technology. We also have the advantage of being able to replicate any replacements that may be required. She was interrupted suddenly by the voice of Pakal.

The voice began to speak but changed almost immediately into verbal machine language.

The Android had entered part of its anatomy into a recess of the ships computer terminal. It had managed to override all the security protocols and was now ingesting vast amounts of information. Pakal and the Android now joined, sought the truth. Why had the transportation failed at its last use? It was a merge of minds and not just one way either, as Pakal started to sing;` we shall, we shall - rock you, - - rock you; we shall, we shall-- rock you. The Android; now also clapping in time to the offbeat rhythm, with a single extended hand on the metallic fascia of the control unit that progressed into finger drumming until Appi demanded it to be stopped, at once, as she glared at Rocco who instantly recognised the look of displeasure.

But he enjoyed this kind of music from his favourite band, known as Queen. He especially liked their version of the Bohemian Rhapsody back on Earth that would certainly have followed, had it not been for the interruption.

Rocco and Appi burst out laughing as the rest of the gathering looked on stone faced and shocked.   Rocco intervened. `Don't worry my friends, we always harmonise with our Androids when we are working on difficult problems. We have liberated our crew to allow them to develop a personal identity. `
As he finished speaking the Android approached them. ` Captains`; It glanced at both. ` I believe I have the complete instructions and a possible reason for the previous failure. ` He paused and looked behind, as though a stealth detective as he spoke the words;   ` Sabotage. ` Glancing again at both Captains, he now spoke as if he were Pakal, in a deeper more severe tone. ` With your Command, I will correct the problem and advise on its usage. ` Rocco nodded, and they waited with the other crew in anticipation for the first test to begin.

Chapter Two

Tepintri the wife of Tuwa, Tonati-uh, Lord of Mayan and its entire people, relaxed in her temple like home. Its design was as the ancients, although not so much a monument, but a smaller compact model of the same style. Outwardly, it mirrored their historic designs and displayed the Mayan hieroglyphic script on the outer walls with the exception that it had no vast stairways leading up to the sacrificial altar and perhaps heaven.
All the old ways had gone, it was no longer necessary to make sacrifice to the gods, only dusting and cleaning the many abandoned deities.
Tepintri, had been directing the servants in their duties and enjoyed some of the minor domestic work herself, tidying and cleaning came naturally to her, more so since her association with Appi. Perhaps she was broody, or something in her metabolism had clicked when, she and Appi had dressed up and done the baby walk at the last party.
She had enjoyed the feeling of heaviness and when they had done the walk together, it felt right until. Well the men, they should have coughed at least, to save her embarrassment. To just arrive without warning and catching the two women doing the strange swaggering actions of walking whilst heavily pregnant was unforgiveable.
Tepintri`s thoughts returned to the celebration, a few days prior; where they had all gathered. They had examined the treasures from the Ja`Way, that Rocco, Tuwa and Appi had discovered after they entered the Space ship for the first time. `They must need some attention. ` She was speaking half to herself and half to her absent husband, a sort of trial lie, to hear how it sounded in readiness for when he returned home.

Her interest was more than curiosity. She had examined the Mother of pearl box and just had to know what it contained.

With these thoughts in mind she went to Tuwa's special place and collected the items that, (she would say) had become dirty and covered with sand, dust and finger marks.

There was no need to coerce Tepintri, she loved cleaning and fairly rushed to submerge the items into a bath of soapy water. She had thought that a thorough clean, would reveal any secret openings or minor fractures on the pearl box, but it only floated.

Disappointed she took up the challenge of rubbing some soapy water on the be-jewelled, golden model, of the Ja`Way. The model was extremely heavy and her delicate, soap filled hands, failed to stop it slipping from her grasp, landing heavily on the pearl box which cascaded into balls of brilliant light and soap bubbles.

 She screamed; the sudden shock and realisation that it had broken, tempted her to run, But on closer examination she could see that the box had actually opened revealing small white square onyx containers. Each box holding a single elegant finger ring, engraved with a Mayan design.

The designs were not unlike a signature ring, known for sealing documents with wax and she could not resist sliding one on her finger to admire its beauty.

The ring surprised her by automatically adjusting itself to her correct finger size, grasping the flesh drawing a little blood as it tightened its grip.

She became a little frightened when she tried to remove the ring and alarmed to discover it would not come off. She lifted the heavy model of the Ja`Way out of the bath and as it passed the pearl box, it closed its lid? This was astonishing. She had discovered that by moving the model over the box it opened and closed. She returned the small empty container back into the box, but the ring remained.

Her panicking thoughts were racing about what to do when she then tried sliding the model Ja`Way over the ring several times but it failed to release its grip and remained on her finger. Her thoughts were now that if she replaced the box no one would notice. She had so many rings surely; Tuwa wouldn't notice this new one. After cleaning and drying the items taken from the bath, Tepintri replaced them back into Tuwa`s hiding place. Now she would have to wait and face the consequences of her actions if when her husband returned later, he noticed anything out of the ordinary.

On the Ja`Way, excitement mounted as the Android declared through the voice of Pakal that they were now ready, and waited for everyone to gather for a display and some initial instructions.

` At the first level, ` the Android announced. ` The one to be transported, would be contained in a single cubicle, (there were ten to choose from.) Then the operating Engineer would select the appropriate switches and sliders to achieve correct destination and ultimately transportation.

Anything in a non-complex solid state such as wood, iron, plastic etc, would not require any special attachments for the machine sensors to recognise.

`However, ` Pakal's voice announced with grandeur. ` I have discovered that for human or carbon based transfer we need more information.  The Android then asked, ` Would anyone like to try it. `

Hushed silence followed. Someone suggested that they try a box or something small first.

A small container was placed in the cubical and with the Androids explicit directions, an engineer made it disappear. `We now` stated the Android. Reverse the switches and sliders and proceed to return the container.

This produced a startling effect in the chamber, a whirlwind of dust and particles circulated   and clouded the interior of the chamber until Tuwa's wife, Tepintri suddenly appeared like magic in the cubical. She was completely naked except for a skimpy pair of panties. Appi stunned by the surprise hesitated, before removing her over jacket while rushing across to cover her friend's embarrassment. Tuwa glared in anger, his face red and going purple. 'Who, ' he began. 'How has this? This will not do, this machine picks up anybody anywhere without direction' He stopped and looked across at Rocco, ' how did it choose Tepintri from all the people on this planet? '

The small group dispersed, to belay their leader's embarrassment, giving their excuses' they all went to another section of the ship to wait for some explanations. It was difficult for Tuwa to comprehend when his wife explained that she had been changing her clothes at home to visit her husband. Then she was here? No one could make any sense of what had happened until Tepintri confessed about the cleaning and went on to explain, what she had done and to her disbelief, as she showed them the ring, it slid off her finger, easily.

Rocco and Appi examined the ring and discovered the impregnated chip within the Jade graphics; microchip recognition the size of a pin head that also controlled the finger attachment device that had gripped Tepintri's tender flesh.

So now it was understood, that the ring was required to use the device and it could not be removed until the traveller had returned to the ship. That would also explain why the container had not come back.

So Rocco, again as usual, stated the obvious. ' There must be another setting for general goods. '

Lord Tuwa was concerned about his wife Tepintri, she appeared normal and unaffected after her experiences but he insisted she needed to get specialist advice and have an internal examination. Rocco volunteered all their services at the medical centre on the Invistor Star which, was accepted with gratitude as all four of them left to go to Tuwa's home, where they would collect all the treasured items found on the Ja`Way before departing on the shuttle.

It was a convenient time to get together, to discuss the intricacies of the transporter; while Tepintri's medical, tests were being carried out. Rocco pointed out that they could use some of the special equipment to study the rings, to establish how it had assisted in her transportation.

Appi and Rocco were secretly pleased to be back in their own familiar quarters. It seemed that they spent more and more time on both of the planets, helping with the daily problems instead of enjoying their own existence together. Appi would spend more of her time preparing for the birth alone. She would like to include her husband in the intricacies of birth and togetherness she was alone and scared of the unknown actualities. She had her mother, but it had been some time since her mother had any birthing thoughts. Her mother seemed more anxious than she did and she had not mentioned it before but there were the dreams that led to actual fear and anxiety, for not only the birth but, perhaps it was the absence of her beloved Rocco, this really frightened her.

One dream had become more frequent and interfered with her catnaps. It was always the same; she would awaken startled, in a hot sweat, followed by the anxiety of losing the baby. It was the repetition of her clone, standing with wide murderous eyes brandishing the large knife while Appi unaware, her arms wide, and   out stretched, waiting to welcome her Rocco.

Each time on waking, she would immediately turn to where Rocco laid to find an empty place, and then comfort herself, by realising that it was only a dream. She would pull his pillow nearer and embed her face, into the centre; just the smell of him gave her reassurance.

The dreams were becoming more frequent now, perhaps because of the changes occurring within her body, as the baby was getting ever bigger.

This nightmare was an experience that she had tried so hard to forget. There came the relief when suddenly, she would realise that she was never alone, nurse chat-a-lot was always near stationed in the corner to protect her, just as Rocco had ordered.

However, since she preferred to be in her own comfort zone with Rocco beside her. This night was a blessing, after all the excitement on Mayan with the transporter, they were here together; she could reach out, touch and smell him. Their relaxed bodies cradled together until he turned towards her and they coupled, slowly and gently into a state of euphoria that lasted until they both drifted off to perfect sleep still joined as one.

A new day dawned on the Star; everyone had overslept after the jollities in the hospitality lounge. They had something to celebrate, Tepintri; Tuwa's wife, had been taken to the medical area and examined by Rocco's favourite Android; nurse Chat–a-lot who had determined that after installing Tepintri into the specially constructed consultant's room.

(A futuristic, heavily shielded, small surgery area. Where, data was analysed after collection; by the very latest radiology devices.   This was an area so advanced, that it could perform technical surgery and minor operations by using computer-generated arms with laser pinpoint accuracy.)

It was found that Tepintri had some unrelated gynaecological problems and when the tests had been completed, the results were translated by nurse Chat-a-lot that the transfer by the transporter had no effect on her at all. But, Tepintri went pale as the nurse relayed new information. She seemed worried about how the rest of the results; how was she was going to explain to her husband all the new diagnosis.

The close nit relations and friends were gathered in the visitor's lounge of the Star and when she arrived, the celebrations were in full swing having already started some hours earlier. This first sight seemed like a blessing to Tepintri because now perhaps lord Tuwa would have celebrated enough to accept her important announcement.
It would be two fold. Firstly, the nurse had been delighted to tell them that everything was where it should be and that the transportation had no ill effects at all. However, from now on they would have to take special steps to avoid any more such excitement.
Then Tepintri took over to give Tuwa his surprise and the biggest shock of his life; when, his wife declared that she had an alien presence inside her.
`Yes my Lord, I am at long last; ` Tepintri's face beaming with womanly pride, `I am in the early stages of pregnancy. `
At first the shock struck Tuwa dumb, but as the refreshments started to take effect, he began to relax more and more until well after the girls had retired to their quarters. In fact, he relaxed to the extent that Rocco had to carry him to his bed in the visitor's hospitality suite.
Tepintri, woken by the confusion of the men trying to quietly open the door, was found standing just inside. She had her arms folded and looked concerned as she helped move her husband to his side of their bed. Rocco assisted by removing some of Tuwa's outer clothing while Tepintri leant over at

the other end, struggling to pull off his shoes when her attire fell open   revealing her beautifully formed breasts that suddenly emerged through the lose silk night ware. She glanced sweetly at Rocco, slightly embarrassed but a little excited that he should be in her bedroom.

 She briefly imagined them together, but tried quickly to think of something else as she felt her face blush.

Rocco showed disinterest, Tuwa was his friend but he noted how beautiful Tepintri was as their eyes eventually met. Rocco eased his friend into a comfortable position and made his way towards the exit.   He whispered ` I am so pleased about the news of the baby. ` Their eyes glazed together for seconds as Tepintri accidently revealed her full beauty, when she took his hand and kissed his cheek gently, releasing her hold on her gown. She was un-ashamed at the excitement generated between them and felt the wetness of desire.

Rocco turned and left with a vision like the first man meeting Venus the goddess of love rising from Botticelli's seashell with a feeling of absolute lust, but he was drunk and by the morning, all the crazy carnal thoughts would have disappeared.

The morning arrived with its usual clatter and aroma of the prepared food waiting in hospitality. Rocco was surprised to find Tuwa sitting alone in the lounge; he had just started his breakfast and gave the broadest grin as Rocco entered. Tuwa stuttered, ` I can't begin to explain how happy I am. I shall be a father and our children will grow together in strength and beauty. ` They were both enjoying the thought when the girls arrived.

Appi was the first to speak. ` You two look like cats that have found the cream`, she then went on to explain the meaning to their guests. Tuwa smiled, ` we were discussing our children's future` Rocco glanced at Tepintri, who pretended not to see. ` It would be nice if they were a girl and a boy` they all agreed.

`Well now` Tuwa said with impatience. ` I am ready to start the new attempts to raise the Ja`Way. ` Rocco had agreed to accompany his friend with one of the Androids ` shall we go? ` Rocco nodded and reminded Tuwa about the rings ` If we have them with us we can at least leave the craft in any emergency. The two wives were somewhat upset that they could not go with them, and showed it but they agreed it was a wise decision. They could accompany them after all the tests and safety devices meticulously tried and tested to everyone's satisfaction. In any case, Rocco reminded them that he would always be in contact with Appi telepathically on the Invistor Star and they would always be in her shadow.

The crew of the Ja`Way were pre warned of the shuttlecrafts arrival and positioned at their allotted stations all in a state of readiness.

Tuwa entered the command centre and immediately greeted by Pakal the guardian.

`Welcome Tuwa, Lord of Mayan, defender of.............. `
Tuwa interrupted Pakal. ` Please modify this welcome to just welcome Captain Tuwa.  This ceremonial welcome intonation is very long and unnecessary every time I enter. `
He paused `Pakal, I wish to be known as Captain Tuwa from now on and the welcome ceremony only to be used with my permission on special occasions.

`Tuwa seemed not to realise that he was talking to a computer projection and gave Pakal the sort of politeness that was reserved for humans. 'By your command Captain;'
Tuwa cleared his throat, `Attention Ja'Way, begin start up procedure. The sudden movements of the ship trembling into life as Tuwa remembered, that they should pull the ship out

in reverse, raising the tail end upwards, allowing the nose cone out of the sand pit.

Slowly with more shuddering the Ja`Way strained until with a sudden jerk it was free and flying backwards at a height of 40meters towards the beach and open sea.

Tuwa gave the order to level off and they slowly cruised away with an excited cheer from the crew.

The ship handled well as they turned from reverse to a forward movement and skimmed along the extremities of the beachhead.

After quite a long jaunt, Tuwa decided to change direction back towards the beach. Ja'Way turned like a giant swallow flying with precision, and the feeling of excitement relaxed until the order was given to reduce speed and height.

They were about to test the ships ability to float. Tuwa guided the ship slowly and gently until she smoothly glided along the white foam of the sea where it began initially to float then, suddenly there were cries from the rear end, where water was gushing into the service bay. Rocco suddenly took command and gave the order; ` Increase speed and height, to one parcet and level off. `

The ship shot up and assumed a stable position. They waited for confirmation then Rocco ordered the rear doors be opened to let the water out. ` He turned to Tuwa, `I would like to raise the nose a little to help with the flow, but I don`t know how stable the shuttlecraft are. We don`t want them to go out as well! `   Tuwa was quiet; he had been slow in reacting. He realised that the position could have been disastrous.

The two Captains moved quickly to view the damage in the bay and discovered it half full of seawater. Rocco was first to speak, ` asking the rear crew if the doors were shut properly on takeoff. `

Tuwa watched and waited as they argued the truth until some information slowly became known that the large tailgate door was closed but there had been a gap with the smaller side door exit.
` Rocc, do you think it was done on purpose? `
Rocco did not reply immediately.
` I suppose there is always that possibility; did any member have a grievance? `
Tuwa did not wish to comment, he could not believe that any member of his handpicked crew would want to kill them all, what would be the motive. It was a prestigious and adventurous start for their first opportunity to travel the far reaches of the Cosmos like their ancestors.
Rocco made a decision, ` Let's assemble all the crew responsible for this rear area, those that were here on duty as soon as all the water has been cleared. Then after interrogation, we will close all the doors up and try again but this time you and I will have our transporter, I mean the chock-winik rings on. ` Tuwa smiled, ` Rocco I think I prefer transporter. `

The team assembled to explain how the small side door reopened after takeoff. They all looked nervous as Rocco walked slowly along the line slowly examining each face as he questioned individuals about their duties. Satisfied that each knew what was expected to do he began to casually amble back along the line then stopped between two men about half way along the line, turned his head back and stared. ` I know you mister; you're that trouble maker, the prophet of doom. ` The man backed away, and then suddenly made a dash for the rear exit ramp where the door and tailgate were still open.
Rocco drew his laser and shouted. ` Stop or I'll shoot. ` But the man knew his cover was blown and he was determined to leave to avoid punishment. The prophet managed to reach the

edge of the tailgate and Rocco fired, blasting the man right out of the opening.

He returned to Tuwa`s side while the crew, shocked at what had happened, waited nervously unsure of what would happen next. They had witnessed a new kind of justice, dispensed swiftly without reason until Lord Captain Tuwa explained about this man who had caused trouble before, inciting the people to riot and now he had tried to jeopardize the whole venture by nearly sending them all to the bottom of the sea.

Tuwa turned to his friend, smiled and nodded. Thank God he thought, Rocco had seen the danger and dealt with it.
He ordered the tailgate closed and the side service entrance securely locked. There was to be no mistakes this time. Captain Tuwa glanced across ` will you stay here a while Rocc, I will return to command. With that, he left, as Rocco watched the crew tidy up the shuttle bay.
It was about five minutes later when the orders to descend were given again. They felt the craft tilt, their nervous glances watching for signs of leaks while waiting for the equalizing pressure to build up once again. They knew, that the ships interior, would crumble if Ja'Way descended too fast. The crew, especially those in the tail section began to relax; they secretly prayed that the Ja'Way would not let them down, while Rocco, satisfied that the danger had passed, decided not to return directly to the command centre, but go directly to the crews quarters and then on up to the Captains.
 His troubled thoughts still nagging him, as he entered the cabin. Rocco prodded the panel with his finger, revealing the secret armoury and security screens.

It was too much to hope that there had been only one person among the whole crew who wished them ill.

 He wondered how the prophet had managed to get on the ship; Rocco did not see him as a courageous individual. Since, he did not actually take part in any of the fighting. Neither, did he appear to be the type, to actually do any pre-planned deed himself; or for that matter any of the dirty work but, like a ravenous animal he fed on the excitement he created, enjoying his power to incite whilst whipping up the frenzy within his followers. Yes, Rocco thought that more trouble may be in store.

He smiled as the security panel screens opened automatically; this was a wonderful device that displayed separate areas where the cameras had been activated by movement. They were situated in the most vulnerable areas of the ship. He spotted his friend Tuwa, looking very efficient directing operations; he had a tendency to conduct as he gave directions. All he needed was a baton.

Rocco noticed that on one camera in engineering someone seemed to be tampering with the transporter mechanism. He called Pakal and ordered immediate connection with Lord Tuwa in command. ` By your command` came the reply.

`Yes Rocc, ` Tuwa seemed a little out of breath, ` what is it ?

`     Rocco tried to hide his nervousness` Please go to engineering with two security guards, as quickly as possible, someone is tampering with the Transporter;` He went on as an afterthought,  ` Oh Captain I suggest we leave the sea now, return to the surface. `

Tuwa picked up on Rocco's voice and ordered, ` return to surface immediately, ` as he ran with two guards to engineering.

On arrival, they found two men actually engrossed in some cutting and rewiring of the transporter. The men resisted as they tried to arrest them but Rocco arrived and within seconds, they were sleeping from one of Rocco's   special holds and dragged by the ankles to a secure lockup area.

On the return to the command centre, Rocco ordered the ship to level off at twenty meters above the sea and directed it to wait over a soft sand area of the beach while he contacted Appi by telepathy and requested that she send their technical Android to investigate what exactly had been done to the transporter.

Tuwa was agitated, ` I can't believe what has happened. These men were chosen especially for their knowledge, trust, and family positions. `

He sat with his head in his hands as Rocco tried to give some words of comfort. ` I believe that we do have some good men here that some have been led astray by that trouble maker, well thank god he has gone for good. I cannot see any other way but to dismiss this entire crew and restart with a new selection. ` He paused, ` perhaps from Sawston's men from Freedom! ` Tuwa stared knowingly. ` Yes, I know your right. My own people have done nothing except to try to kill us. `

Rocco nodded, ` shall we find a nice soft landing spot on the sandy part of the shore and begin again? I think that when this team learns that we only want the very best and most loyal, their attitudes will change. I will help you choose; if you wish. I have a test that will show their true courage and devoted spirit to the ship and their commander.

Pausing again Rocco went on, ` you know your previous choice of crew was more of a command rather than asking for dedicated volunteers, prepared to serve with their lives. `

Sawston and Awotz met the Captains at the tailgate, after their successful landing on a perfect spot of soft sand just a short way ahead of the beach.

 Rocco studied them closely and said to Tuwa, ` these two for example they should be with us, they are true, dedicated and have a family. ` It was a point that had escaped them they had something to live for. `Yes, yes exclaimed Tuwa. ` They will help us choose and from now on we use only family orientated, experienced people. `

Suddenly Appi and Tepinti came into view arriving from the village they had joined with the other two wives and accompanied by the master Android who passed without pause going directly to the Ja'Way.

The small gathering of the Captains and friends waited for the crew to re-assemble on the beach for further instructions. Tuwa called them closer together and ordered that the prisoners be brought from the cells for interrogation. He wanted everyone to witness that they were fair and any judgment he delivered would be deserving and more to the point just.

Rocco organized the collection by a telepathic message to the Android and security Drone working in engineering.

Tuwa continued with his prepared statement. ` Some of you men will be aware that today, saboteurs tried to sink the Ja'Way and kill us all, not once but twice. `

He looked angry and his voice plainly showed his disappointment as he spat out the words.

 ` We do not know why!  Neither do we know if this is the final attempt. ` He went on. ` We suspect there is a device on board that could explode within the ship. ` Another long pause, as he glanced at Rocco, now indicating that he must wait.

Rocco had received a message from the Android and Drone. Which, he relayed to Tuwa. ` Lord Tuwa, the two prisoners have killed themselves in the security area, ` he paused, ` by hanging. `

Unfortunately, the security Drones had neglected to remove their belts and laces.   Tuwa was outraged; they had denied him his revenge and the opportunity to prove to the rest of the crew how they had all been lied to by the prophet and leader of the sect.

As Tuwa studied the faces of the men gathered before him he realised that they looked to him for leadership. He must remain calm and show fairness since many would naturally be related in some way to the conspirators; recovering his composure. Rocco continued. ` These men have taken the cowardly way out and there may be more of you that feel the same, for all of these reasons, I am taking the precautionary steps of disbanding the entire crew.

There was a pause and a shuffled murmur within the ranks. ` Anyone found in or near the Ja'Way will be shot immediately without exception or warning. ` This brought moans of dismay, many of the crew wanted to stay, work, and fly with their Lord Captain.

Tuwa turned and looked across to Rocco a small group gathered and started arguing as to who was to blame for the attacks and damages, punches were thrown and scuffles started between them, while the majority slowly faded away to return to their villages and families.

Lord Tuwa put on a brave face as he invited his friends, their wives, and their families to his home to enjoy refreshments and discuss ideas.

 It was a sort of get to know you party come meeting and ended very amiably with the feeling of friendship enhanced with the new partners from planet Freedom.

Chapter Three

The following morning Sawston with Awotz and a party of men from Freedom arrived and paraded at the front of Tuwa's residence, with them came a group of six volunteers from the surrounding Mayan village.
It was quite a show and Captain Rocco was asked to address them.
` Gentlemen I would like the married men to assemble on my left, `he indicated with his raised arm. Those now grouped on the right please leave your names and details before leaving, we will contact you later.

The men remaining were given a detailed explanation about the capabilities of the Ja'Way. It was then explained what would be expected of them after they had gained experience and trust. The new crew would be required to
learn special skills and gain the same qualifications as members of the previous crew.
Obeying orders is upper most they would be expected, without question, to follow their commander.
 He went on into more detail, ` this ship has a device that disassembles our bodies and reassembles them again anywhere within several parsecs, ` he coughs; ` we don't know its actual range, yet. `
Tuwa intervened and explained all about the transporter or Chock-Winik in their own native language. Which followed by having a discussion and a break for the men to consider all they had heard so far.
With everyone fortified from refreshments, the group reassembled to hear what they would be expected to do and Rocco was called to elaborate. ` In a few minutes you will be asked to experience this dangerous and complicated transfer.

Of course, this is voluntary and it will show no reflection on anyone that prefers not to try.

'So,' he smiled 'those that agree to try please remain where they are and everyone else wait on the right hand side. This caused quite a stir and really confused the situation. Some took the left hand side and then changed their minds to go to the right. The same occurred from the group gathered on the right, and between them and their indecisions they produced a whirl of dust, as they all turned in circles, forward and backward until the larger party was standing on the right who gave their names for future appointments.

The assembled more courageous and dedicated men, were led by Rocco to the engineering area where they were given rings and neck lets for communication. Then they were directed to the waiting cubicles.

At this point only one man bottled out while the rest including Tuwa and Awotz arrived at the beachhead and waited for the second batch containing Sawston and Rocco, who brought laughter, as he stood nervously ridged for quite a while, waiting to see in case anything dropped off.

The others were amused to see him nervously unbuttoning the top of his trousers, `just checking` he smiled.

`Gentlemen, ` Lord Tuwa had got into the habit of addressing the crew at any opportunity. ` We can at last state, with confidence that, not only do we now have a way off in any emergency but, a team of the bravest men on this planet.

In time, we will appraise the work that you do and test your capabilities. ` The atmosphere was now ablaze with anticipation as Tuwa continued. `After training I will then appoint sub- commanders who will have the complete responsibilities of running each section. `

With that, he waved his arm and gave the command for them to be returned to the Ja'Way and within minutes, the ship had raised itself to a great height, while the watching families and spectators cheered.

Rocco at this moment thought of the ill-fated Titanic back on earth and wondered if he had done the right thing in insisting that he travel with Tuwa and the new recruits.

He smiled at his friend to give confidence while behind his back he crossed his fingers.

The Ja'Way performed so well that the actual age of the craft seemed completely unimportant and not one member of the crew questioned it. Rocco thought that it was perfection itself as she cruised through the outer atmosphere into the vacuum of space closely followed by The Star, as a rescue back up ship.

The air of excitement cleared, and the women now seemed assured that their husband's chances of survival were increased to at least seventy percent. They had a team of dedicated family men willing to achieve and had studied the recently documented knowledge of the Ancients and their advanced space technology.

 Appi's chief Android, had worked hard on deciphering, not only the transporter but also the detailed mechanics of the ship and had printed out many pages of translations into Mayan. The following days of testing and manoeuvres had given Captain Appi the opportunity to study procedures with her beloved Rocco on the Ja'Way and enough confidence to leave the ship with Tepintri who assisted her to the shuttlecraft. She did not want to use the transporter because of her condition.

Tepintri had witnessed Appi's pain; she had seen her reach for the guardrail as a twinge of pain from the baby made her cry out.

She now insisted that they should watch the Ja'Way expedition from the comfort of the Invistor Star and keep a red alert not only for the last trial runs but also for her and the baby just in case.

As the shuttle left the Ja'Way and Mayan as Appi again felt discomfort and Tepintri advised that she should relax, even lie down after all that excitement; it couldn't be good for the baby.

Appi agreed she was quite big now and near to her time. She could not be sure whether she was six or seven months making calculations difficult especially when she knew that on her planet of Moofee, the gestation period was on average only seven months.

The shuttle's arrival on the Star was met by nurse Chat-a-lot and an un-scheduled scan was made when Appi passed the nurse Drone, as she was ushered to the surgery.

It had been her intention to visit the medical section for investigation only, but nurse had deduced and mentally telepathed to her, that her time was close and the baby would not wait.

Chat-a-lot had arranged everything. It was, as in the modern Moofee way. Appi would be installed into a clinical chamber, where the entire process of birth could be assisted and monitored under a special anaesthetic that is incorporated in the jelly like substance that, she was slowly being imbedded into. It was like a womb within a womb. The Moofeeians considered this to be the most practical and pain free system, where the mother and child could exist together within this artificial womb for the entire birth.

Tepintri waited anxiously as Appi twitched within the chamber, her naked body trembling with nervous reactions from the movement inside her. She did not seem to be in pain but it was difficult to believe that all this could happen while totally immersed. Then came another strong spasm and the room was cleared.

Back on the Ja'Way, Rocco also felt pain and suddenly everything before him became pink as he stretched out grabbing a monitor unit to steady himself while his vision cleared. He suddenly realised communication was lost between himself and Appi and he received a message from the command centre on the Star that was now following behind in the wake of the Ja'Way.

The chief Android spoke to Rocco directly, he politely asked for instructions, stating that Captain Appi was incapacitated and had retired to the medical section. Her last requested was that he return immediately and take command.

Rocco shuddered, 'This would be a first. 'He thought, ' A human transfer from two moving space craft at this speed. It would be far more dangerous than he had anticipated; he would have to transfer in flight from one craft to another using the newly acquired Choc-winik transporter. ' Oh God ' He murmured; Rocco could not show fear to the crew and after all they had recently used the device, so without hesitation he arranged to collect the Mayan ring with the neck band communication device and instructed the transportation section.

However, Tuwa did not want to take the risk and ordered the Ja'Way to stop for the Invistor Star to pull along side.

The risks of such a transfer while moving was unknown and could they thought, either have resulted, in his re-appearance within a wall, or even perhaps be melded within a solid object. They knew that their inexperience made it impossible at this time to fix a safe target area for him to regenerate in.

It was agreed then; they would aim for a largish area and they made the transfer that thankfully was successful.

On arrival he went directly to Appi's side but as he approached he was shocked to find himself barred, locked out of the medical area.

Nurse Chat-a-lot approached to remind him of the basic Moofee directive that, ' no males are allowed during the delivery procedures. ` She declared that he should not worry. Captain Appi was in good health and had excellent attendants all under computer supervision.

He had rushed for nothing, Appi would have to put her trust in Nurse Chat-a-lot, they surely would manage and she would call him when their child arrived.

Rocco suddenly felt completely lost as the nurse prodded him with her extended metal finger and he moved sideways towards the guest area where Tepintri was patiently waiting.

 Her big sad eyes drew him close into her space until they embraced taking warming comfort from their clinging bodies pressed together, squeezing away any doubts and fear that they had for Appisommati.

Both could feel the warmth seeping through the thin seasonal clothes they were wearing and Rocco realised just how potent Tepintri was as he felt her hands slide slowly down his spine to its lowest ebb, gently pulling him so tightly against her that he could feel her mound of Venus gently moving against him.

He did not resist as they just enjoyed the moment without kissing while Rocco's thoughts raced, his mind working overtime, imagining them together and this time, it was Rocco that could feel wetness as he pulled away.

He knew that she wanted him and perhaps he would live to regret it but, he could not betray his true loves trust and only hoped that Tepintri would admire him for it rather than hate for being rejected in her wantonness.

They parted slowly and Rocco entertained her with small talk and soft drinks as they waited in the lounge both trying to explain but neither understanding the delivery techniques or the exclusion of all males, during the strange Moofee maternity rights and baby delivery.

It was late when they retired and his thoughts again turned briefly to the embrace; his pangs of guilt, and secret thoughts, that he could betray his beloved Appi. Rocco talked to himself in the mirror as he studied his brow looking to see if any horns had appeared on his forehead. `We will have to leave this place. It is the only way. `

He was scared and thoughts of a woman scorned came to his mind. ` No, ` if they were ever to be truly happy without the temptation, there could be no other answer.

Rocco truly admired his friend Tuwa and could not deny that he had strong, very strong feelings for Tepintri.

But, the real adoration of his life is his beloved Appi, they were inseparable and now she had given him the greatest gift of all that would bring them even closer to share everything.,

` My God` he thought, and repeated ` my child; and I haven't even thought of a name!........

His thoughts wandered off into sleep and he dreamed again of all things wonderful that slowly progressed into a more sinister crazy dream of tenderness with Appi that led to explicit sex that took him to the point of no control.

A fever would not stop. After each explosion of satisfaction they returned to the beginning as if a new reawakening.

She brought him again and again to climax as her whole body trembled with ecstasy from multiple orgasms each time they plunged together, both shaking with unfathomable pleasure sinking into the deep chasms of frantic oblivion, until eventual exhaustion brought it to a head and he awoke in the arms of ' Tepintri ! '

He was shocked, immobile and completely under her spell, unable to even move a muscle as though bewitched, while she again consumed his vital juices bringing his sensations back to a peak, while working her magic on all his erotic zones, to the point of total submission.

There seemed no end, she had drained him totally of everything; he had no reserves. This was an all night unbelievable session that had left him completely dehydrated, drained, feeling as old and as wrinkled as the fabled Methuselah.

Ching, ching, ching, ching...

The alarm sounded again, for the second time, its unusual sound still simulating a knife tapping on a wine glass until the glass shatters that brought him back to full alertness and the realization that the room was empty he was very alone. He checked the adjoining quarters and shower area. No entry had been made, before or after he had retired, it had all been a fantastic dream.
He stood between rooms unable to think straight, but the alarm brought him back, emergencies should come first as he hurried to the Command centre where Rocco discovered that several large ships from the Coalition of planets, had gathered around the Ja'Way.

It appeared that they were contesting Tuwa's rights to enter their acclaimed area of space surrounding the other planets.
Rocco did not want to intervene since Lord Tuwa and Sawston were together on the Ja'Way, both being the recognized leaders of the two outer and only other colonized planets.
The remaining planets, a huge white dwarf and three others were deemed as uninhabitable and quite unsuitable.
Nothing of any value had ever been found there. In fact, no one had ever lived there, according to a recently discovered document of historical records.

Rocco ordered the Star into a position that flanked the other ships; he now had an unimpeded view and could easily control the situation, just in case they started another unprovoked attack on him and the Ja' Way.

He strode across the main floor of the command centre to view the outside situation, and noticed an armada of smaller craft coming from the planet Freedom. Then joining them at a distance, were the Mayan fleet of shuttlecraft.

`Full alert` Rocco ordered ` this could be really nasty. `

He watched as all the smaller craft, took up a posture of defiance.

They then split into two groups, both moving into a position that could control both the outer flank and rear of the column, it was stalemate.

Rocco was directed to an incoming message that was being transferred to Command and dashed to listen to the translation being relayed to all the fleet.

The voice of Lord Tuwa came clearly through the speakers; it was tense as he explained the situation was heated but they were having diplomatic discussions and that the deployed craft surrounding them should remain calm until further instructions. Then, privately he spoke to Rocco, he requested that his wife Tepintri should stay where she was, on the Invistor Star for safety and he promised to re-lay any change to the situation, during the progression of the talks. `Don't worry my friend, I will keep in touch. Nevertheless, its times like these that I wish I had the facilities to converse directly to you like Appi and you have. ` Rocco was secretly pleased that Tepintri would be around.

His secret hopes, were that she was responsible for the fantastic nights of indescribable pleasure; but in his mind the truth was, it would end in tears. However, every man had a second brain, stimulated by his dick and his secret fantasies.

A man would willingly die of a pleasure so great and that he would give, his very soul for the same regular abuse, believing that it would constitute the true meaning of life, be it on Earth or elsewhere.

Rocco left the command centre; he wanted to see what progress Appi had made but nurse Chat- a-lot was on guard as usual and would not allow access declaring she was still in the delivery chamber. There was nothing that the frustrated Captain could do, except make a detour on his return to see Tepintri and give her an update of both situations.
He had hoped that she would be waiting for him in her quarters, but, she had already left and he found her sitting quietly in the visitors lounge.
Again, those all enveloping eyes met his and he felt the colour in his cheeks change. She just looked ravenous, with a smile that indicated more than just friendship.
`Are you very tired` she asked mischievously, ` how did you sleep? ` He grinned. I'm fine thanks, I slept very well indeed. How about you? ` Tepintri Yawned. ` I started out very restless; I'm not used to sleeping alone, ` she smiled, `
but later I fell asleep and had a wonderful dream, she stretched her arms as her face showed nothing but, a little pink flush that said everything. She purposely stared at him, as she licked her lips, her eyes penetrating deep down into the dark corners of his inner thoughts.
 `I couldn't eat anything for breakfast. ` This time a cheeky knowing grin appeared.
Rocco was totally intimidated; he had spent the whole night alone yet could not understand why he felt that he had exhausted all his life giving energy.
The butterflies in his stomach did not help; this woman could stir him by doing nothing even though he could hardly keep his eyes open.

The day passed slowly with messages passed and advice given between Tuwa and his new friends within the Ja'Way crew. Sawston meanwhile, sent his compliments and requested a meeting for later the next day.

He thought that their communications were being monitored. Then abruptly concluded; that he felt sure no easy Diplomatic agreement was going to happen in the very near future.

The long awaited evening arrived, the talks were still going on when Rocco retired to the lounge, his beloved Appi was still comatose in the chamber, and Tepintri had already retired for the night. Rocco could not wait to get to his quarters and retire as well. He was so exhausted that he just fell onto his bed, too tired to even remove his clothes.

He slept almost at once and dreamed again as the night before. He and Appi enjoying each other's bodies and telepathic thoughts that became deeper and more exciting as they explored each other's secret areas of eroticism.

It was as before, again nonstop frantic climaxes until both exhausted, and drained, as morning arrived.

Rocco dragged his weary body to the lounge area for breakfast, physically and mentally exhausted. He was drawn, and unshaven yet, his guest seemed full of spring as she looked across the table. ` Did you have a busy night? ` She asked as she ran a long finger nail down the front of his chest.

He grimaced, ` difficult to tell, I had an early night but awoke exhausted. ` She quickly replied ` Did you sleep alone? ` He laughed, ` well there's only you me and lots of Androids? ` He didn't smile and there was no answer.

It was much later in the day when Sawston arrived and immediately they went into conference about the discussions. It was plain to see that the Conglomerate had big ideas, and it was not just the space between the planets, that they wanted. The planet Freedom had many interesting resources that the large mining companies were eager to get their hands on despite all the overwhelming odds. It was as though this party of businessmen could not understand that the two nations had made a pact and were now joined in partnership and close friendship.

The new Coalition between Mayan and Freedom had really brought everything to a head, because suddenly after all these years they had been offered unrestricted knowledge and a goods exchange trade that achieved more within the last few months than in all of the previous two hundred years.

The Conglomerates still believed that the partisans of Freedom were slaves, still ignorant within their little handmade shuttlecraft that had expelled so much radiation that it nearly killed off the whole race.

Sawston was angry, and exploded for the first time against the interlopers. `When would these slavers realise that they could not frighten his people anymore. We are strong now and they must reckon with a long lasting peace that will be kept for as long as I live. `

He went on, ` I intend that now we are free, the two nations will go from strength to strength and have hope to continue until we also achieve a Star ship status. ` Rocco raised his hand, `you know my friend, I really like you` Rocco had something he wanted to say. `You are a promising politician, God, I am glad we are on the same side. Between us on another day and another subject, we could beat them all. However, I am desperate for sleep and I can't understand why? You know, since my arrival to be with Appi during this difficult time, I have been unable to sleep. So, ` He yawned, a very long yawn. `Let's both sleep on all this and

we can talk again at breakfast in the morning. ` Turning to leave he remembered.  ` Oh, I have arranged for you to be near my sleeping quarters in case we are needed in a hurry. Please consider yourself at home my friend and help yourself to anything you need. This Drone is at your command. `
With that, Rocco practically ran towards his quarters and hit the bed so hard that he was asleep before his head hit the pillow.

Chapter Four

Very early the following morning, something had disturbed him as he glanced at the time display it was not an hour that he had expected to be found wide-awake but totally refreshed. He showered and thought thank God he had not suffered a single disturbance or dream during the night and was it seemed, back to normal except he was ravenous for food and liquid.

Quietly leaving his quarters trying not to disturb his guests he crept along the passage way and suddenly felt the hairs on his neck rise as something moved fleetingly along the surface of the corridors side wall, down towards to the visitors quarters where Tuwa and Tepintri had their accommodation

It had no shape or texture as it floated like a steam shadow gliding against the textured finish.

Whatever it was, it had not detected him, and for the first time since leaving his home planet Earth, Rocco drew his hunting knife from its scabbard.

It was seconds later when his knife imbedded itself into the side panel wall and the shadow vanished under the nearest door that was adjacent to Tepintri and Tuwa's quarters.

Rocco gave a telepathic alarm to security as he withdrew his knife. He was sure that he had not missed and examining his blade there was nothing except a taint of colour from the wall and a clear oily substance.

The area was cordoned off, while Rocco used his skills and bypassed the doors locking system and stealth fully entered the room but found nothing.

A special device was brought from the science laboratory that registered vapour and gas detection. It was an application they had for any Gas and liquid faults within engineering, but still they found nothing except that on leaving the room, he noticed a tiny glistening droplet of clear liquid under the door.

On Rocco's instructions, one of the Drones collected the sample and delivered it with his knife to the ships laboratory. The security alarm was then cancelled, but he did set a low yellow alert and ordered a careful watch on all areas.

Strangely after all the commotion, neither Sawston nor Tepintri appeared and thinking that they had slept right through he continued his way to the breakfast area and devoured an enormous meal of all his favourite things.

`My God ` he exclaimed `I really was starving, all that energy and loss of sleep ` He turned, to a slight noise just as his friend entered the room. Sawston smiled and said `I seem to remember that talking to one's self is a sign of extraordinary sexual appetite my Captain `

He looked a little drained and went on to say that he had, had the most extraordinary night and could not explain why he felt so hungry. ` I never eat anything in the mornings, but today, please fill my bowl. NO, I mean fill my whole tray with food and drink, they laughed together as they chatted and amazingly, Sawston went back for more!

It was some time later that they were joined by Tepintri who looked stunning, like a young bride. Both men acknowledged her and she did pink slightly in the face as they admired her perfect womanly shape. She asked if they had slept well, then mentioned that she had an unusual headache and that this morning she would only order a drink before joining her husband in the Ja'Way.

`My Lady ` Sawston coughed as a small partial caught in his throat, he stood up to clear it and chocking fell towards her. Tepintri outstretched her arms in recoil and they fell together across the polished floor collapsing some chairs and a small coffee table. Rocco rushed to her side and saw that his friend was turning blue. `Quick `he shouted ` he's choking` as he turned his friend over into the foetal position while inserting two fingers into his mouth and throat it made Sawston throw up and the object was ejected with a flick of one of Rocco's fingers.

With the help of a Drone, Rocco carried his friend to one of the large lounge chairs and helped clean him up while the Drones cleared away his breakfast remains.

`Oh my God ` exclaimed his friend, ` you have saved me and they both turned to address Tepintri who was still lying on the floor.

Her upper attire was torn across the chest and arm with a large amount of undigested breakfast food spread across her peeping bra.

Rocco again rushed to assist her and advised that she had better go and change after a wash.

She allowed him to assist her back to her quarters and it was a short time later that, he realised while she was actually changing that, they were again alone in her chambers, separated by a door that remained ajar while they were talking. It seemed the most natural thing as she composed herself and removed the remainder of her top clothing. He noted that, there was some bruising on the arm, and a substantial cut, that required treatment. Nurse chat-a-lot was summoned immediately.

Rocco was very concerned; his admiration for Tepintri was painted all over him in great big florescent capital letters.

She did not seem so reluctant either as she stripped completely and disappeared into the shower area. It did not seem to matter that he could see her, she could feel that it turned him on and as she re-entered to dress she stood momentarily facing him in all her glory exposing her perfect unsupported voluptuous breasts. However, Rocco had seen it all before and now in his imagination he was trying to assess how that deep cut had occurred.

~ 43 ~

The Mayan people and their ways were still a huge mystery to him.

His thoughts were wondering if the Mayan's had mystic capabilities with spiritual and bewitching charms.

In his imagination, his dreams came to the fore, as he remembered how it was that he able to feel they were together, when the room was empty. Then, a noise at the door distracted him, followed with a whoosh of it being opened that made him turn and the nurse suddenly appeared to attend Tepintri's wounds while Rocco reluctantly thought this an appropriate time to leave.

He returned to the lounge, to find Sawston shaken but recovered, waiting for his Captain. The two sat together regretting the incident discussing the details. That led on to his friend elaborating on his restless night. Rocco listened intently as Sawston told how he had retired a little after Rocco had left the evening before and although not quite immediately, he had thought about his wife and family. It was strange, that in his thoughts led on to remind him of their early courtships and exciting nights after the wedding.

Then his dream became wild and more exciting, it seems that it had lasted all night until he had heard some noise outside their quarters. However, he was unable to rise, too exhausted, even to turn over, and gladly returned to slumber until deep sleep followed.

As soon as Rocco heard this, he was alarmed and started to explain what had happened to him stopping just before Tepintri returned to the lounge. She ordered refreshments and smiled as though nothing had happened.

` I hope I haven't missed anything` she didn't seem concerned.   'No, no, ` uttered Rocco ` we were just discussing how we could make it up to you for destroying your dress. ` He lied, not wanting to frighten her.   She smiled sweetly at him again.

Sawston jumped in at this point and apologized profusely ` I was about to say earlier that I would be returning to the Ja'Way today, and would offer you a lift.

Although your husband, Lord Tuwa did mention that you may be staying here for a while until negotiations had been completed. `  She answered with a ` No, I have learnt that my friend Appi is now very close to producing the baby and I am no longer needed for assistance, so I would be pleased to return with you. Perhaps my;` she paused.   ` Lord Rocco could come and collect me again later.

Rocco nodded, he thought the pause at my Lord said a little too much.

Chapter Five

The afternoon arrived and Rocco now totally alone was fast asleep on a couch in the lounge when, the Invistor Star alarm rang out chinking again and again.

The glasses crashed and he was not sure which way to run first, should he go to the surgery to Appi or to the Control Centre. A voice came to him from control

` Captain we are picking up another very large space vessel on our advanced long-range monitors. It will be here in a matter of forty minutes.

The alarm brought the real reality that another planet had become interested in the new order of business between Mayan and Freedom.

Rocco, arriving at the command centre half expecting to suddenly be involved with an aggressive confrontation and was surprised to find that the new space visitor had taken a position at the rear of all the small shuttlecraft from planet Freedom, whereby closing the gap between the planets.

The Conglomerate ships were now trapped and the negotiations took on a much more subdued argument of rights and threats.

Lord Tuwa had nervously contacted Rocco about news regarding Appi and also his concern about the new arrivals, although at this time it was uncertain as to who they were and Rocco suggested that they use this factor to their advantage and say that they had also shown interested in trading. After all, who wouldn't? This made Tuwa laugh and he said that he wished Rocco could join him, but he quite understood.

Now suddenly the communications section of the Invistor Star, contacted both Command and   Rocco, to inform them that the new craft was in fact a Moofee Battle cruiser called

The Aparsuent   and their Captain was asking for permission to join with the Invistor Star.

Rocco was both surprised and delighted but he feared their reaction to him, because he being not just aboard their craft but, also the Captain. It may cause some friction after all he was the intruder. Still these were Appisommati's people and he had to meet them at some time.

However, in retrospect he felt that it may be a blessing, perhaps they would give him the opportunity to learn more about them and help him meld in with their customs and attitudes before he reached Planet Moofee and Appi's family.

Rocco was informed of the docking, and all the procedures that were to take place in the shuttle-docking bay.

He was astounded to find on arrival all that the Androids and Drones lined up ready for inspection. It seemed that it was a red carpet affair, without the carpet of course but as soon as the shuttle landed all the Automatons stood to attention and made a sort of piecing whistling noise that (to him) sounded like a comb and paper salute.

Then some music played that could have been their National anthem as the door opened on the shuttlecraft.

He assumed correctly that the Captain would be the first to alight and he took up a position at front edge of line. Rocco then walked to the head of the Drones and bowed extending his hand, which was accepted and vigorously shaken with the broadest smile he had ever seen.

` I am Captain Pilot Spansetgar; I am please to meet you. `

Rocco had some difficulty in retrieving his hand back.   `

Captain, I am called Rocco Townsend, I have command today because our Captain Commander is in dispose. `

He did not want to go into the explanations of why or that she was having his baby.

Then another whistling from the whole complement of Drones but, this time with gusto and an elderly man and woman joined them and introduced by Captain Spansetgar.

`This Captain is Diplomat Lord Duvan Adberry and his wife Lady Appisommati. `
Rocco went completely ridged as he stared at the Lady and his mouth dropped open as he realised it was an older version of Appi. Her mother!!   ` Oh My God ` he exclaimed.

His face went bright red and he was stunned to disbelief until a voice behind him quietly stated.
`These are my parents Rocco. ` He turned on his heels and there before him in all her glory was Appi carrying their baby cradled up in her arms. He rushed forward to embrace her with a multitude of kisses and took the child to his chest forgetting all about the distinguished guests.
Suddenly all the presentations went completely to pot as the parents also rushed forward and without hesitation made a group hug, even Captain smiley did not escape and then to cap it all into a perfect day, all the Automatons began to applaud, their clapping extensions echoed throughout the shuttle service bay.

It was the most fantastic scene, the women crying and the men hugging and laughing at the unimaginable.
Rocco thought, ` thank God they didn't start singing that Queen song of `We will rock you!
Rocco turned to look at his beloved wife; it had been some time since they had been together. He whispered in her ear of love and `Is it a girl? ` He nervously asked.
She nodded and produced a large roll of paper with a special red seal, which he held like a royal command for all to see, he opened it and read aloud.
` This registration document is a legal and binding affidavit that certifies that the small person you are presently holding is our true production and your daughter, to be named April, Appisommati Adberry Townsend. If you find this name agreeable, it is therefore declared and hereby given as proof,

is my bill of expenses for all my services in the production of said daughter. `

The tears rolled down his cheeks with laughter as he went on to explain that they had broached this subject many times before and he had been warned that she would present him with a bill.

The group went on to the visitor's lounge where light refreshments and a million questions were exchanged.

Appi's parents were exceedingly friendly and seemed genuinely pleased with the new son in law. Rocco was amazed that they already knew much of the pre-history from the computer log files that had been transmitted by Command to Moofee.

Later that evening, they were all invited, to the Battle Cruiser Aparsuent where a beautiful banquette had been arranged. It gave the happy couple the opportunity to invite and introduce their close friends from Mayan and the planet Freedom to the family gathering and exchange cultures.

Lord Tuwa was in his element; in fact, he seemed to be quite merry describing all that they had gone through together from the arrival of the Star, the discovery of the Ja'Way and the treasures that they found aboard it.

Rocco had lost count, of how many times the story of the Drone had come up; the excited laughter about the Drone actually walking outside the shuttle on the roof, with the white flag.

The happy couple were exhausted, especially Captain Appi. They wanted to be alone on their own ship within their private quarters. So, they quietly stole away having decided to retire early with their baby daughter who as yet still had to be introduced and bond with its father, Rocco.

They left the festivities and Rocco was again light-headedly in heaven with the two people that he truly cared for, his only prayer was for an uneventful early night, of peace and happiness.

It was slightly after their arrival on the Invistor Star and their entry into the main passageway that followed on to their quarters. Rocco saw the scar on the wall where his knife had pinned the shadow and it reminded him of the laboratory analysis.

This he thought would be his first action on the morrow but for tonight, he would insist that nurse chat-a-lot should continue to remain in her alert position close to all of them.

As he lay on the bed with Appi it seemed like the very first time, when they had been together laying side by side and now seemed slightly surreal with little April between them as he reached out and gently lifted her onto his chest. She lay with her head to one side with her arms and legs spread like a turtle. He could feel her little heart beating and the gentle rhythm of her breathing. Appi moved closer alongside to Rocco the picture of perfection they slept so soundly they did not hear or feel nurse chat-a-lot gently adjust the bedding and secure little April into a cushioned valley position, protecting her between the two Captains.

Rocco was the first to raise his head and watched with fascination as April edged herself over the cushions and found one of the nipples in the valley of Appi's breasts.

He watched, as Appi did not awake but instinctively repositioned her body to allow full access to both of her swollen nipples.

Rocco slid gently over and out of the silk sheets, he listened to the smacking sound and murmur of contentment while he dressed and quietly exited the room.

It had been a quiet, undisturbed night and he was totally refreshed to the point of humming his favourite lucky tune as he entered the lounge to find a surprising guest already having breakfast.

Awotz stood as he entered and they greeted with the usual handshake. Rocco waived the formalities and poured himself a hot drink.

`My Captain` Awotz began with a serious and concerned look, ` My Captain before my family and I took our leave from the wonderful party last night, I spent some time with my friend |Sawston. Please understand, what I have to say is unproved, a fable perhaps, but I could not forgive myself if anything happened to you or your family. `

Rocco looked bemused, but Awotz was never a man to tell tales and Rocco relied on his straight forwardness. He trusted this man and prepared always to listen intently to anything he had to say.

He continued with the story his friend and leader Sawston had related about the wonderful night he had on the Star with Rocco and the amazing reality of his exhaustion the following morning after a visualisation and an encounter that lasted all night and left him feeling so weak that he could hardly get out of bed. The experience scared him and yet now, he found it difficult to believe that any dream could produce such realism or do what it did to him.

Rocco watched his face   ` I also had a similar dream not once but three times, each time the realism became more profound more aggressive more erotic; to the point of total exhaustion and total submission.  I was, as though drugged unable to move. ` A silent pause, ` yes my Captain this Sawston also told me, it scared him, he also thought at first, that he was tied to the bed. `

They stared into each other's eyes and Rocco went very quiet ` Awotz my friend you have heard or have seen this before? `

` Yes, I have heard but not seen. There is an ancient myth of a spirit that came at night like vampire but it's not for blood; it sucks the life away in stages of extreme pleasure. The ancients called it smoking cloud,
(K'AK' MUYA) `
Rocco went white and rigid. ` I have seen it he whispered, let's quickly go to the science laboratory, I have some samples. ` They left discussing how Rocco had obtained the sample by pinning the shadow to the wall and he hoped the analysis should give some indication of its makeup and what could be used against it.

Their arrival at the lab had caught the Drones in an unusual confusion, they had made many experiments to establish the makeup or DNA of the samples and apparently the discovery of an unknown liquid that was a derivative of fish oil but contained a great deal of testosterone. They had deduced that this creature could also hibernate since some tiny cell fragments in the sample showed it had the capability of reproducing minute amounts of testosterone that could perhaps be used during an induced survival period, when its natural food was unavailable.

The unexpected calamity now was that the Drones had tried to save the sample by freezing it with liquid Nitrogen, but unfortunately, it had accidently destroyed it.

The Chief Techno Android now gave a computer-generated deduction from their analysis of the small sample. `This specimen`, it began ` was from an unknown creature or species. It appeared to survive as a gaseous form, which had the ability to alter its structure and metabolism to be able to feed mainly on spermatozoa, from which it must extract testosterone. Its main supplier would be the male gender of any living species. `

Rocco seemed deep in thought, and then asked ` Would it be possible to reproduce testosterone synthetically? `

~ 52 ~

` Yes ` came the answer almost before he had finished asking the question.

Yes Captain, the chemical formula is: - Carbon, hydrogen, oxygen, Calcium, Zink, Magnesium, and Potassium. ` Stop, please stop.  We know the main formulae for life.  ` Yes Captain. `
The Android turned collected and returned the Captains knife.
`Well ` Rocco started, `this is going to be interesting; somehow we must arrange a trap. `
He smiled while he mentally compiled a message and telepathically conveyed it to the Android with specific instructions.
The Android acknowledged that it should produce the synthetic substitute of C.H.O. He thought that a quantity of what two men could supply at a single sitting would be sufficient for their purpose, and it should be stored very carefully.
Rocco turned to Awotz, `now my friend, how is it going to be arranged. `
Awotz thought that in a container that could be sealed easily once the entity had entered but it may be necessary for at least one person to be in the room with the container.
`I wonder how intelligent the shadow is.  Rocco pondered. `It seems to be incredibly tactile and extremely knowledgeable, of the human form. So I surmise that it would not accept a dressed up Drone as a living male, even if we covered it in artificial skin and layered it with tons of smelly male perspiration that extruded from some artificial glands. ` That made Awotz laugh, `no, you're right, one of us has to volunteer while the other controls the trap. `
Awotz interrupted, `what if we use a male animal, a large male pig, yes. That is a good idea, but this entity has much knowledge, I do not think a pig would fool it. However, we

should keep it in mind if the shadow was hungry, it could work. `

Awotz turned smiling and made a statement that shook them both. ` What if there is more than one!  Mmmm, better get several pigs just in case! ` They laughed.

`We don't know much about this entity do you think there is someone, anyone on the planet Mayan with this kind of knowledge or experience. `

Both suddenly jumped, and together they shouted,   ` Pakal. Of course, we had completely forgotten, he was around before the problem started. `

Rocco caught his breath, `I am going over to the Aparsuent to bring my new father Lord Duvan and his wife. Could you go to the Ja'Way and see what Pakal has to say. ` Awotz nodded.

During Rocco's return from the dual visit and Appi's parents, with Captain Smiley, they were cordially invited by Lord Tuwa to his home.

They had suggested that they would like to visit the area where the Ja'Way had been found during that fated beach party which led to the exchange of stories about their return to and from Earth.

Rocco enjoyed his revisit to Mayan but his mind was on the information that Awotz would bring. He was restless now and even the short explanations with Tuwa seemed to make things worse especially when Tuwa requested a meeting with all four of them. As the party developed, Lord Duvan and his wife expressed an interest in seeing many other areas of the planet, with hopefully other planets, because the Moofee community had been searching for a new home. A habitable planet similar to their own green paradise, that was presently being affected by a great white giant ; that threatened to go super nova in the not too distant future.

The gathering seemed to get on very well they appeared to enjoy each other's company so much that the thoughts of their present dangers had completely vanished into the jovialities as the wine flowed but all that changed when Awotz and all the men disappeared to closed rooms.

Lord Duvan accompanied the men and listened with intense interest. He had never heard of such an entity and after the explanations of all the happenings, the meeting went to a new level when Sawston and Awotz added the latest disturbing information.

They had both attended a meeting with Pakal in the private security room of the Captain's quarters on the Ja'Way while Lord Tuwa was still discussing terms of business and the exchange of manufactured goods between the six planets.

The party of men now sat with concerned faces as Sawston began by saying that their meeting with Pakal had given plausibility to the Shadows existence. They had discussed this race of entities that were well known in the earliest colonization's, as shape shifters.

((This caused an immediate reaction with Rocco, He choked on an intake of breath, his thoughts racing immediately to that night when he and Tepintri had laid together, she inducing untold pleasures in that sexual nightmare.

 Now he understood; the shadow, had taken the shape of the only unencumbered female on the Star.))

Rocco recovered slowly but managing to continue to listen to the rest of Sawston's information.

`They were the indigenous inhabitants of Mayan their original name (K'AK' MUYA) or smoking cloud a deception they employed as an escape by altering their appearance to a shadow.

Unlike us, they survive like the ancient tales of the un-dead or vampires but here, they do not kill intentionally since blood is not their elixir of life. We now know, thanks to Captain Rocco's near capture of one and the laboratory tests, that it is, Testosterone from spermatozoa and since it is so much more difficult to obtain, they prefer to harvest their supplies from several male donors who are kept by the explicit sensual enjoyment of sex. This is an exchange that is unsurpassed by any other form of enlightenment.

It is thought, that this present Shadow may not be the only one.

We think that it may have been transferred to the Ja'Way during the initial tests with the transporter and somehow brought aboard the Invistor Star by accident.

It has the ability to paralyze with a mild anaesthetic then feed at its own convenience, perhaps something like a leech once attached. `

Pakal had explained its heritage as a sea dwelling phenomena that the ancients used for self-gratification

`And` (Sawston laughed nervously) `it's probably the over excess that killed them. `

A voice from the door, interceded as Captain Spansetgar entered `I wonder how we could communicate; do you think it is possible?

 I am sorry I am late Gentlemen. `

Spansetgar had taken the opportunity to investigate the total computer knowledge, available on his ship the Aparsuent, while Awotz had interrogated Pakal on the Ja'Way.

Rocco grinned at his new friend as he took up his position around the table, he couldn't help it. Captain Spansetgar always reflected a broad friendly grin and had now been dubbed the name of Smiley, by Rocco.

`Gentlemen, ` Rocco announced, `this special meeting has been called to eradicate the pest, now known as the Shadow. Until now, no one had considered the possibility of communicating, with the floating entity. ` Someone uttered, ` where would you start? ` Awotz took this quiet gap to mention what had transpired, during his meeting with Pakal on the space ship Ja'Way earlier that day. ` Pakal said that the Shadow had been around during the Ancients occupation. They must therefore have recognition of some of the original language. ` `But`, Sawston cut in, ` Where have they been all this time?  Do you really consider that they have a secret place and hold another community captive?  A community that regenerated the Mayan species, without anyone seeing, hearing or realizing anything! `

`Oh My God` Tuwa suddenly exclaimed! ` We have been so busy off the home planet; I discarded a strange happening that was relayed to me. ` He stopped and drew a crumbled cloth from a slit in his over shirt and wiped his brow. `

Rocco, when we raised the Ja'Way and took off on our trials, it was reported to me, that a hole had appeared beneath the original resting place of the Ja'Way. I ignored it then, it was a couple of days ago and we were so busy at the time.

Anyway, this hole, has now totally collapsed and there appears to be a shaft, a perfectly circular shaft?

It has, been hidden perhaps for centuries.

` He went on ` Oh my god, could it be ?..........It would explain the situation of the ship, it's strange position and depth, the missing crew, why the transporter was sabotaged when they realised that not just the crew were leaving but perhaps the Shadows may have entered!`

The room now completely silent all deep in thought of the implications when, suddenly the door crashed open and everyone jumped practically out of their chairs as a small child was retrieved by Accra the wife of Awotz who smiled apologetically while dragging the wide eyed child out of the room.

` That's it ` cried Tuwa, `we must capture one preferably a youngster. We can then negotiate if we have something they really care for. `

Another voice deplored the idea, ` surely that's the worst thing we could do, to steal a child!

The discussions went wild on the who's, how's and wherefores until it came back to language. No one living on the planet's surface knew the ancient language. Then it was suggested and agreed, that perhaps only a Drone, would be able to ingest all of Pakal's knowledge immediately.

So, it was unanimous; they had decided that a Drone would be prepared in the ancient cultural arts and languages of all the original Mayans and they would try to make communications.

Chapter Six

Rocco approached his new friend Captain Smiley who was talking to Lord Duvan. ` Thank you for your input and ideas ` he began. ` I thought that when Appi and I left my planet Earth, we would be sitting in the command centre of The Invistor Star enjoying the passing Cosmos. I never imagined such wild and strange happenings everywhere we go.

Lord Duvan had not spoken much at the meeting, but now saw the opportunity. ` How do you think the people on your planet would react, Rocc? ` He used the familiar term for his new son.

`Ah Sir, you are not, I hope putting me into the same category? He smiles, ` I am sure that they would explode their latest atomic weapons and kill everyone and everything without thought of consequence.

The reality of other peoples and extraordinary entities are presently beyond human; not so much belief, but certainly Psyche or patient understanding. On Earth, they still imagine that they are alone in this vast universe, believing they are undefeatable and still aggressive even towards their own kind.

I dread to think about what they might do if they ever obtained such power and technology that, we carry. The history of the Earth is traumatic, from the very beginning nothing but Wars. The latest; bigger and more devastating than you can imagine killing millions of people and all other forms of life.

Even I have been drawn in to do despicable acts to survive. ` He stops. ` Please forgive me, It is my deepest nightmare. Rocco sees the effect his honesty has upon the two men. ` I'm becoming a party pooper let's go for a drink and join the ladies in that order.

`Rocco, what's a party pooper ` enquires Captain Smiley.

`My dear Smiley, it is the name given to those that always think the worst, making everyone else, unhappy no matter what the occasion.  Now, in your case I have given you a new name that reflects all the things I like about you. ` He turns to Lord Duvan, `what do you think Sir?

Duvan laughed, yes your right, I now wonder, what name you have allotted to me. ` They all laugh as Rocco ushered his new friends and family into the main reception area of the Star where a commotion had started between the guests about the contents of the special meeting called to discuss the (K'AK' MUYA) or Shadows.

Rocco noted that in some areas of the room, some more speculations had emerged about the large ventilation shaft. He heard the words ` found underneath, ` and then ` the last resting place of the Ja'Way back on our planet, Mayan.

Somehow, the two items had become associated into the same frenzied discussions. Someone then mentioned the maps discovered on the Ja'Way and the possibilities of finding the ancient underwater city that may contain more treasures and the remains of original descendants of Mayan.

Rocco's thoughts turned to how all this speculation had arrived from so little information, he smiled to himself this was incredible and had to shake his head when he heard that now someone had started them into believing that they may have been cohabiting with the Shadows.

` God ` Rocco shouted,

` Lets get this into prospective ` and poured himself a strong root drink recommended by Tuwa.

'You know Tuwa; I think we should compose a message.............. `   But his friend was being pulled away and into another speculation that made Rocco instantly construct a message in his head and mentally sent it with instructions telepathically to the communications section on the Star. He then ordered the chief Android to broadcast all the prepared transcript of the ancient translations throughout the whole ship.

His hopes of confrontation grew as he heard the strange noise of the messages quietly echoing into every dark corner of the Invistor Star.

He felt that his previous intimate meeting with the Shadow would encourage it to make contact with him, again.

Later that evening Rocco had found himself alone with his thoughts. Appi had gone with her mother and father to their own ship and all the visitors had departed to their own quarters set up for guests.

Somehow, in deep concentration he had wondered away from the visitors lounge and into an unused room far away from everyone else. It was a room, which he had set up as a study, a private den, where he had made some of his best decisions in the quietness that was respected by everyone as a no-go area.

It was therefore more than surprising for him to be disturbed during these quiet moments of un-interrupted peace by Lord Tuwa's wife Tepintri.

She had entered so quietly that he had not realised her presence until she sat beside him.

She seemed pale and worried as they stared into each other's eyes. He could see that she had been crying and that her whole demeanour showed pain and discomfort.

They did not speak but both just sat and listened to the audio message faintly playing outside in the corridor.

Rocco was the first to relay his thoughts. ` You know Tepintri; I truly hope we can express our thoughts with this life form. We mean it no harm as long as it does not interfere with our natural way of life.

I understand that in the early history of this planet the ancients and the life form we call the Shadow lived in harmony.   There is no reason why this could not be re-instated again? `

Tepintri did not speak as she now moved closer and took his hand in hers, it was unusually clammy and had a rough texture that made him suddenly realise this was not who he thought it was.

Tepintri was the softest, smoothest, and cuddliest woman any man could wish for.

This was remarkably like her but he wondered now, if he was in danger.

Rocco continued to maintained the intimacy between them, he did not want to alarm her, while in his head he alerted his communications Android to announce a special message in the preferred language of the Shadow through the computer hardware on his study desk and over its speakers situated in his den.

`Please do not be alarmed, ` the voice whispered from the computer. ` My name is Rocco and I would like to talk with you and meet with your community. `

The girl did not pull away but looked in the direction of the computer and gave out a weird noise that sent a cold shiver down his back. Her response was re-laid via the microphone to Android communications who translated back to Rocco.

`I know intimately who you are; we have already joined. ` She smiled as he responded with a facial flush that put embarrassment itself to shame.

` You are very different to all the others and so clever to search our language. I should have realised by your very beautiful responses to my touches. Please, let us make talking instead of loving. `

Rocco, regaining his composure, started to related the facts about his inquiries into their languages and the K'ak'Muya relationship with the Mayan people many centuries before. She nodded and added, a screech that hurt his ears and then translated, `as it was, is now. `   He must have looked shocked, but continued, ` Now, that we have met and I understand how you must make, ` he paused, ` human satisfaction, to procure the nourishment for your very existence.  What are the possibilities of our two communities being able to regain peaceful co-existents once more? Can it be arranged? Who can organize it? `

He waited for the translation to stop and went on.

`You see we have now discovered a way to synthetically re-produce the ambrosia of your natural needs. `

She now stood and moved slowly away. ` What about human female outlook, ` she screeched, ` I do not think your females, would accept such a proposal?

That is the main reason we all went underground, to prevent the killings of our species. `

Rocco, a little taken aback, ` I have not heard of this?

Do you really think that is what happened all those years ago? `

`Rocco, ` she began,   as she sat again facing him directly. `
Not so many years ago! These happenings were recorded and passed down, through the lines of our re-genitive families.

It is well known how the Mayans hunted us for sacrifice when, we would not comply with their wishes. We are Sea living communities taken for enslavement after the Mayans found out about our powers of changing shape. It pleased them to show us off; they used our needs and special skills for their own gratification.

Later, when they discovered, we were able to not only replace their women, but could physically withstand the torment of their imagination and the ferment of their exceptional desires, our ancestors found themselves in a desperate situation.

Their only way out for us to survive was to continue to do what the Mayans wanted or die from either hunger or masochistic torture that always followed with sacrifice to their new Sun God. `

He waited for her to continue.

`This eventuality nearly brought about their own destruction not only by their wanton excess, but the female of your species could not accept the rejection of their own men. What followed, after the eventual deaths of so many men through this excess and ultimate decease, actually depleted the community, leading to a great outcry and the start of our destruction. ` She paused.

` We are now, only a few, driven to live below the surface of the planet with access to the sea, because we dare not return to our natural habitat.

Rocco totally appalled from what she had said. His mind raced ahead thinking of how to find an answer that would satisfy all parties. `I believe, that we have the means to manufacture everything what you need and with this, I had thought it may be possible to reinstate friendship within the communities. `

The meeting was interrupted, by a Drone; gently tapping on the door. Rocco turned and called, but continued talking with his guest. ` You know I have no idea what you are called . `

`Kak-Maya ` she replied.

No, no that is your tribe's name. ` What are you called? `She shivered as if she was shaking water off a furry exterior. `

You know my tribal name!! ` She smiled, ` my name is Ix-Chel and I am a member of the Ixi-kore, a tribe that live well within the security of the inner city.

You mentioned a production, a synthetic potion. `

The Drone had now entered with a tray of liquids and a message from Mayan the home planet.

Ix-Chel the shadow had moved toward the tray of liquids that had been placed on a large container that was firmly fitted to the floor, ready for travel.

She seemed to smell the liquid contents with a curiosity of a wild cat, as Rocco turned away again to receive the message.

Ix-Chel listened to the translation as he read out loud, ` a party of Mayans searching for a lost child have found a small shoe at the perimeter of the ventilation shaft, they believe that the child has been abducted but, it is possible that it may have fallen down the  open shaft. `

Turning back to explain the details to Ix-Chel, he grinned to see that she had moved much more closely to the tray and was just trying the first samples of the contents.

A long purring guttural sound trembled from her lips. There was no translation, (how could there be) but, she knew exactly what it was and looked at him in a different more admiring way.

` Captain Rocco ` came the translation, ` what you have discovered in this synthetic potion is the secret of our freedom. It seems to be just as enriching as the real thing but

lacks just a little condimental flavour. Not bad for someone who has never tried it!`
`Ha` he retorts grimacing, ` and never will. `

They returned to the seated area where Rocco elaborated on the message, explaining about the mysterious shaft.
 He went on to discuss what she thought they should do after suggesting that they should return together to find the child before the villagers take any crazy action.
As he finished his explanations, he realised that the time had passed more quickly than they had imagined. Suddenly it became three O'clock in the morning and certainly no time for him to retire to bed.
`How do I pass you off as one of us? ` He paused, while scratching an irritation on his ear, ` you can't continue as you are, Tepintri's husband will be with us. `
He paused again, ` Can you take on any form? `
Ix-Chel's beautiful dark mooneyes enveloped him. They swallowed him whole and he could feel his resistance weakening as she deployed and demonstrated all of Tepintri's charms that he admired so much.
` Rocco, I can be anything you want but; after twelve hours I need to feed, recuperate my losses, and recover all the energy I have used.   They sat quietly until he asked, ` What form would take the least amount of your energy? `
Ix-Chel quickly disclosed that, ` a snake would be the easiest but I prefer to travel with you as a Mayan, I trust you and truly would feel safer by your side. `
He nodded and agreed. `Let's do that.

What else do you think we need? `
She looked thoughtfully into his eyes again and whined a new sound that translated into a soft appeasing request
as though, they had known each other intimately all their lives. `Can you arrange for my new nourishment to be with

us and we will need lots more extra examples of the elixir to show the elders of my tribe.

He laughed heartedly, ` Of course I have already arranged a large quantity to be made and stored in frozen containers that will be available tomorrow. I mean this morning. ` Rocco paused as though looking for the words he needed. ` Ix-Chel, I do not know your normal form, or how I should know the difference, between the male and female of your species. Is there anything I must know and not do for etiquette? ` Ix-Chel seemed not to understand the question and perhaps wished to avoid the subject as she watched his eyes slowly begin to close and spent what little time left studying his face, as she lay quietly beside him while he slept .

Two hours later a small party departed from the Star and travelled down by shuttlecraft to the planet.

Rocco had not discussed with anyone his plans or that his new companion was actually a shadow who would accompany him.

Dawn was breaking as they arrived and some of the villagers had assembled at the landing area.

Lord Tuwa was greeted again in the usual manner; it was as demanded by the ancients, a full ceremonial, without a red carpet but with all the officials in attendance.

His lordship despite his protestations could not get the dignitaries to suspend the service during any of his unannounced visits.

This time however, it was urgent and stopped abruptly as the party quickly excused their haste, by swiftly speeding on towards the last resting place of the Ja'Way.

On arrival, they found a picket guard had secured the opening of the ventilation shaft and after some intelligence updates from the Star and the guard, they made an inspection of the shaft rim where some hand and foot holds were found descending deep down on one of the chimney's sides.

The group gathered to discuss the plan of attack and after what seemed a long heated consultation; they agreed that Rocco and the Mayan stranger would go down first and investigate while waiting for the Drone to be lowered on a lifeline.

Tuwa and the others protested strongly until they witnessed the stranger increasing in his height and structure, suddenly becoming much taller taking a more menacing and aggressive stance.

It was strange that only one person; Tuwa, queried why the unknown Mayan, was so suddenly an important member with the group, he also asked why this man accompanied the Drone so closely and why the necessity for only them to go with Rocco rather than himself and his close friends.

Rocco smiled and tried to console the situation, he could not explain anything now. The Drone, must accompany him for protection. He did not say however that it was their only interpreter or that he was unarmed.

This was a difficult position for Rocco, he had a promise to keep, and his explanations were quirky with the exceptions that the group now knew that they were the backup and he needed his trusted friends ready and able to defend against anything that may come out from below.

The team knew his leadership had brought them all together not only as friends but also as leading members of the alliance.

Rocco raised his hands and apologised to his friends while explaining that all would be revealed later.

He really did not have time to explain the reasons now why his small party had to go first but, he managed to convince the party that, if he did not send them a message or return after five hours. And; (He smiled) if they still regarded him as a true friend, the team should follow his lead with weapons.

In the mean time if they could assemble some means of making their returning ascent easier, that may also help the child if it is, still alive.

They shook hands and as Rocco offered his to Tuwa he whispered into his ear, ` I am with the shadow. `

Then they climbed into the shaft carrying backpacks and hold alls quickly following the stranger Ix-Chel before anyone could stop them.

Tuwa was annoyed and showed it, but he respected his friend's intentions suspecting that Rocco was being forced into making these actions. However, Tuwa had assured him that they would be joining him no matter what.

Those left behind, Sawston, Awotz, two crewmembers and Lord Tuwa decided to erect a scaffold across the shaft to enable a counter weighted lifting device with two large baskets. Their idea was that in one basket they would assemble many large rocks that would make the descent and raise the other basket with occupant.

It meant of course that one person would remain at each end to equalise the loads and at the end, they could pull up the last person.

Awotz and Sawston had privately spoken about using the Ja'Way teleportation device; it could certainly reach the bottom end of the shaft. However, they were unsure about its capabilities of penetrating through any obstructing rock, what its maximum penetrating distance could be, through such volcanic substances.

Above the planet, the new ship Ja'Way had now moved its position closer to Mayan; contact had been made by some of the crew after joining them on the surface using the transporter.

Ix-Chel and Rocco had reached the first section that led to an area where they had a choice of three directions. As he waited for the translation to finish, he discovered that if they had taken the wrong tunnel it would lead to their death.

 It was a security trap, which had been left by the Ancients to deter the frequent visits from the surface dwellers. Apparently the tunnel had been pre-set to allow entrance with convincing signs and used pathways, to convince the unwary that this was the correct way but, they would suddenly discover hidden spring board traps, placed in strategic positions that when trodden on would produced a potent gas.

Rocco carved his name to mark the start of the correct tunnel with an arrow for the following team and just in case the need arose in the future for any emergency.

After some 500 meters, the small party came across some transportation that resembled a dual monorail system. Each cushioned or supported by some sort of single magnetised rail. He supposed one for going and one for returning. The floating platforms were inter connected and could be modified to carry more trailers and passengers if required.

He noted that as Ix-Chel followed them on the carriage she gave it a good push and the seating platform picked up speed increased by its own momentum.

The whole system was so simple; the only control, a lever that raised and lowered the platform acting as a break.

Once the magneto had kicked in, they had to hold on to the handrails as the carriage generated its own power, lighting the way ahead.

Ix-Chel had retained her human form and chauffeured them deep into the depths of the earth at an alarming speed.

The system was perfection itself because no matter what direction of travel, once the starting push had been performed, the carriage would float at speed in any direction.

Perhaps the only drawback was that at the beginning of the journey, the tunnels and surrounding areas were barely visible until after at least two kilometres when, suddenly they entered the outskirts of a vast city that was flooded with light showing ancient monuments and Mayan style pyramids.
In the far distance, Rocco could see a terminal stopping place that appeared to have several glass covered tubular vehicles waiting. He was surprised to find the area completely deserted, and as Ix-Chel whispered a sound of anguish, ` this is unusual to find no guard or even a sign of her people. ` She ushered him and their metallic Drone translator, towards the new looking carriages.
They appeared as though they had just been built with a stylish oblong shape that was obviously designed for speed.
The glass topped domes gave an all round visual that would allow them to see everything as they travelled even though they would be fully enclosed.
Rocco noted that the vehicles seem to run on the same principle as the open carriages except that now instead of a handle to lift and lower the carriage for stopping they had a series of hand button controls and a slider that regulated the speed as well. He wondered why they had such an elaborate personal control in each carriage but that (he was told) would reveal itself in due time.

Chapter Seven

On the surface, the team were receiving updates through the Drones, and their transmissions indicated that they would need more time then they had allowed.

Realising that Rocco may have considerably underestimated the time, two hours had passed already and Rocco was still travelling.

Lord Tuwa now took the initiative to consult his team members and they had reasoned that perhaps they should leave earlier but a new concern arrived when a message was received from Appi and Tepintri who had locked themselves into the security chamber on board Appi's parents ship the Aparsuent.

Lord Duvan and Captain Spansetgar, now known as (Smiley) had woken to armed boarders who had tricked their way onto the ship by carrying supplies.

The Captain was held captive in the main control area of the ship while the rest of the passengers had the indignity of being woken from their slumbers by a handful of mercenaries and marched to the lounge while all the quarters were searched.

Captain Appi, had already been made aware of the intrusion, by her personal Drone. She collected little April with her friend Tepintri and they had all been led to safety by nurse Chat–a-lot.

Appi had sent a message to the Invistor Star and with the aid of her Android reduced the intruders by two as they had attempted to capture them leaving her quarters. She also arranged another of the Drones to be sent to the shuttle bay to guard the area and prepare for a strike back at the intruders.

Appi had remembered what Rocco had arranged when her old ship, the Grey Invistor Star docked at the moon base near

Earth. She remembered Rocco explaining what had happened when they had sent the crew over to attack and she wanted to set up the same arrangements.

In this way, at least the weapons would be collected and hopefully the intruders would be made secure behind the applied security screens.

On her instructions, the Star and the Ja'Way had arrived and manoeuvred into a position of defence cutting off any escape by the intruders while members of the Ja'Way were transported to the rear of the Aparsuent where the women were waiting.

Rocco had nervously listened to all the communications from above and had tried to get Ix-Chel to understand that they have to return to the surface. After some difficult explanations, she angrily accepted that everyone on the ship was in mortal danger and that his family had to be protected. Nevertheless, Ix-Chel screamed at the Android that despite the efficiency of the transport they were in, it could not be stopped until it reached its destination.

Then to calm the situation she started to try to explain that there was another exit through the Seascape but at that point, Rocco suddenly learnt the reasons for the carriage controls when they crashed through a portal exit and deep into the sea.

Ix-Chel then reset the controls to arrange the mono car to extend hidden arms beneath the carriage so that it did not lose its connection with the rail. The sea water now inexplicably mixed with another device beneath them sped the craft on, exceeding all other previous speeds continuing to increase until the external view became a blurry haze.

This was no longer a fun ride on a big dipper as Ix-Chel, Rocco and his Drone sat in darkness, the journey seemed endless as they huddled together unable to initially see each other.

As the journey progressed, the darkness in the carriage, lifted a little and although Ix-Chel seemed nervous and unable to speak, he could just make out her features that seemed paled.
Perhaps it was because of the battle between the strength of the sea against the little mono craft and the vibrations from the rocking external forces of the depth combined with the whiff and hiss of compressed gas and air that stabilised the great pressure within the carriage.
They had unwittingly sat holding hands throughout the timeless darkness until suddenly they emerged into an area that engulfed them in brilliant light.
Ix-Chel continued to hold his hand and arm as the transport slowed down and she assisted him out of the carriage as it trembled to a floating halt.
In the extreme glare it seemed to him as though they may have exited from the sea into the sunlight of the planets outer extremities, the atmosphere was hot with a cooling sea breeze that totally disorientated him and convinced in his mind, that they were no longer underwater but above ground.
Squinting with pain, through tortured eyelids, desperately trying to avoid the glare of powerful lights, Rocco stumbled and missed his footing. He nearly fell before Ix-Chel caught his arm and dragged him back to her side. They stood embraced for a second or two her arms tightly holding and squeezing him against her, giving him time to recover his wits and balance.
He listened to the sounds of her shrieks and squeals that seemed to be a warning; until his Drone companion quietly translated.
` We ` she began; ` we have arrived and this is the centre of our metropolis, it is called Ixikore the same name as my

tribal descendants. ` She paused. ` In a few clicks of time, your eyes will become accustomed and return to normal. Then we can announce our intentions and confer with the elders of my tribe. `

The smell of the sea, was all around him; it was strong of fish like the smell of a fleet unloading their catch onto the quays of a fishing village. He could taste a slight salty flavour on his lips, but again, he was deceived as he realised he was being very gently coerced into a kiss by his companion, who had taken the bodily shape of Tepintri once again.

`She is so cunning, ` he thought ` she wanted to take advantage of his disability. Her femininity so subtle it initially fooled him until he reciprocated to the softest, sweetish lips found only in a young man's first dream of love.

Then, the dream was rudely awakened, by his nearly walking on some of the creatures that scurried below around his feet while he tried to stabilise his sense of balance. Then something struck him from behind a blow to the back of his head brought him to his knees, he felt the blood trickle down and around his neck as he collapsed.

The Drone went immediately into protection mode and sprayed bolts of lightning to all the surrounding creatures that were getting far too close.

It stood over Rocco protecting his body, not even allowing Ix-Chel to assist him.

It had been foolhardy of them to expect a welcome from her tribe. After all she had disappeared and been thought dead. How were the creatures to know that this man had saved her life and that she had returned with an elixir that would set them all free?

The atmosphere became heated and Rocco's Drone had sent a message to the surface that he had been attacked and was lying injured. It seemed serious as some elders attracted by the noise had arrived and tried to calm the situation. Rocco was out cold and needed medical attention to stop the bleeding.

Ix-Chel spoke to the Drone and asked it to allow her to assist her companion and move him away from the crowd that had now gathered, surrounding them.

She went into hyperactive mode explaining to some Elders the purpose of their visit. `This man has come to help, despite the odds he had found a way to communicate in their own language; he had discovered a way of helping the Ixi-kore Nation. `

The listeners appeared not to believe what was being said until suddenly, Ix-Chel became taller and more aggressive as before, but now it was to her own people. `We must give him some trust; he is the first friend that we have had. `

She tried to explain above the noise and threats that she, had brought him, she had offered him security, `that is why we are alone. This man's companions are waiting at the great chimney ventilator. ` She screamed ` If they should come now they would take great vengeance. `

She went on to explain that Rocco was not from Mayan and had the weapons to exterminate the entire planet.

This announcement seemed to cause just the right anxiety to get the Elders together and into action.

They moved all the screeching bystanders away. Allowing access for Ix-Chel to attend to his head wound. She had just finished cleaning him up, when another Drone materialised and took up a similar posture of defence.

The crowd screamed in terror at the apparition and withdrew immediately; falling to their knees, they had never seen such a thing. `This must be a God, the Drone translated. `

Ix-Chel dragged Rocco further away and administered water that she found from a nearby dwelling, she administered a make shift bandage to stem the blood, as Rocco came slowly back to life. He discovered with shock that the dazzling artificial light had completely fooled him, they were still under the sea; inside a domed structure that appeared have infinite depth in all directions.

Raising himself to the standing position, the crowd prostrated themselves even lower and it became obvious that they were now in the centre of a city, standing right in front of a golden statue that was perhaps of an ancient deity from the Mayan Empire.

Unsteadily he looked at his blooded clothes and asked if he were seeing double when the second Drone informed him of the emergency on the Star ship Aparsuent.

Tuwa and the team (apart from two local men and another Drone) had already left the planet to assist Captain Appi and protect his wife Tepintri from the fighting.

This was grave news, enough to make Rocco want to leave immediately.

The second Drone had also brought enough transporter rings for them all to travel and after explanations to her Elders, Ix-Chel had also insisted in helping.

She recruited another shadow, an elder of the tribe, who had remained with the gathering to hear the whole story of Ix-Chel's adventure.

How she had vanished during a security visit to the great ventilation chamber where voices had been heard echoing from above. She relates how she had found herself in a strange chamber of whirling dust and sand and the strange happenings that compelled her to change her shape into the cloud and eventually discover how clever these people were in making contact and discovering their willingness to help, the discovery of the elixir and now the trip to find the child.

They deposited the serum elixir that they had brought with instructions to a senior Elder of the tribe who understood from Ix-Chel's explicit directions that they were expected to sample the spermatozoa with the other senior members of the tribe. She demonstrated its attributes and perfection by replenishing herself first. It had been some considerable time since she last ate or taken any sustenance.

Her genuine pleasure of consuming all that was offered seemed to excite the watching Elder, who had volunteered to go with her and made it obvious that he wanted to try the samples and showed surprised that transferred into making those guttural purring sounds that Rocco had recently begun to recognise. He now understood this to be how the Shadows showed great pleasure. With a wry smile, he then explained briefly to his Drone, that it should translate to the present members of the Council of Elders that he expected them to help with a compromise by searching for the missing child and returning it to the surface. He would in return recommend that they could start peace talks and not only supply the elixir for their needs but also give them the means to make their own.

Ix-Chel screeched something that this was the original reason they had entered the great chimney to find the child. The Elder that had agreed to accompany the group now showed some frustration and stated that they knew of no such child, in fact they had had no connection with the Mayans for as long as he could remember. The Drone continued to explain what the Elder said. `The only missing member was one of their community; Ix-Chel. Who has returned to us this day?

`However, it was  agreed that a search would be started within the confines of the City. ` We are a close community and we dare not leave our sanctuary. ` The Elder continued. `
The law is strict and to break it, would not only invite death from the outsiders; but, also incur the heaviest of our own penalties, which are the strictest that we can impose for leaving the city limits.

On the Star ship Pursuant, Appi met members of the Ja'Way as they materialised at the rear of the ship and as Captain Commander, she took control by immediately securing the area and transferring two men to engineering. She then waited for contact from the Invistor Star where upon she ordered several Drones to shuttle across and set up a special reception in the shuttle bay for capture and interment.

Apart from this area, all the other exits had just been closed, when the arrival of new information carried by the Invistor Drones informing Captain Appi about a shuttle that brought the uninvited terrorists, had been destroyed during an attempt to leave.

This was sad, not because the loss of life was unnecessary but the loss of another useful shuttlecraft was always regrettable.

Captain Appi had now contained most of the ship; they had to either negotiate the release of the prisoners or just take a chance and smoke everyone out. She wished secretly that Rocco was there, but he had managed to send a brief message that he would find a way as soon as he could.

The intruders, unaware that they were trapped, had made several demands. They were selecting a number of guests who, they announced, would be executed if their demands were not met. They also implied that this would continue until the Captain complied, by giving them the Aparsuent Star Ship.

Time was running out and only a few of the intruders had been collected and interned in the flight deck area.

Then Appi had a brain wave, she took one of her Drones to the science laboratory and discovered from questioning a resident Android and science technician, that by mixing several combinations of recommended drugs they could produce a gas that resembled, Etorphine a synthetic opiate derivative a special military sleeping gas, discovered during their last Moofee campaign.

The proportions had to be exact since it was known that this gas is instantly effective, it simultaneously knocks out everyone when administered, but if mixed wrongly it would instantly kill any carbon-based life form.

Appi was prepared for the risk, she could only administer this gas to the internal air conditioning that should take care of the guards holding the passengers, and she would telepathically inform her parents and tell them what to do.

The command centre however, was on another separate system designed this way for just this sort of attack and of course, they held Captain Smiley captive.

He would be aware of what's happening and would have to wait until all the others had been safely put away.

The human members of the crew that had been assembled at the rear were given masks along with Tepintri and little April who practically put her whole head and shoulders inside.

Then on command, they all took their positions ready to rush in after the Drones and all of a sudden it was all over, the gas had knocked out everyone, the weapons are removed and fresh air re-circulated.

All the intruders were secured after being escorted to the shuttle bay where, they joined the others who were still recovering from the gas effects.

The passengers now completely recovered thanks to Appi's warning, were able to hold their breath long enough to escape the after effects of the drug.

Rocco had listened to the communication from his wife and was now more relaxed that they had overcome the main problem with the guests but they still had to get command of the ship and while the command centre was, being held they still could be in trouble. `If only they could slip an Android into the chamber. ` Appi's thoughts seemed to be stagnated for more ideas until her father asked about the transporter? `Couldn't it be used to send in two Drones? `

This Appi thought was a wonderful idea but it would need the skills of distraction. This would take some thought. How to distract these people behind closed doors. The first thing out of the ordinary and they would immediately suspect that they were up to something.

No, it had to be a double bluff. But first, she had to move all the passengers and any un- necessary personnel, across to the Invistor Star as quickly as possible. Then a fast run to engineering to disable any communications and reroute the command power supply.

 This meant that she and her Chief Android could control at least the movement of the ship.

The leader of the terrorists had warned them, that they had set up explosives within the command centre and would not hesitate to destroy the ship and their Captain.

A bluff perhaps but they would be aware that the minimum penalty for piracy was incarceration for life or more probably a death sentence for the leader.

They knew that they would be better off to take their lives with the ship and all those aboard.

Appi, thought about the consequences for a long time, she had reasoned that the gas would not be a good idea in case any trigger for the explosives, had been arranged to work with a pressure release control that covered any attack or sudden unexpected unconsciousness.

She had gone over and over in her mind, how they were to achieve the impossible when suddenly, a warning alarm went off, that indicated some people were arriving by transporter.

Appi rushed at once to witness the materialisation of Tuwa with some strangers, then again, the alarm announced transportation and her husband Rocco arrived with friends who just smiled while he hugged his beloved. She asked about the bandage and the head wound as he removed the bloody cloth.

` It's all right Appi; I just knocked my head down in the city getting out of the transportation. My friends here put the silly cloth on. `

They embraced as he whispered to her that all was safe now, they had a plan and she should go across to join the others on the Invistor Star.

As he turned to leave, she felt the tingle of his aura; his secret thoughts came to her as his mind projected his feelings of love, tears of anxiety welled up at the want of him; as she imagined the touch of his caress on the nape of her neck that made her physically shiver.

His last thoughts, that he wanted her safety and she should leave now, he needed to know that she and little April would be safe and waiting for his return.

The small party move away to go forward, toward the command centre, and took up a position outside the entrance where, after some preliminary thoughts and instructions Rocco managed to open a channel to the pirates inside.

He listened to their demands and explained that they were prepared to discuss terms for the release of the Captain and all the prisoners held below.

The Pirates agreed to allow them in but only two could enter and must be un-armed. With that accord, they heard the outer doors click and the two strangers having already liquidised their metabolism into shadows disappeared like clouds of dust beneath the tiny outer and inner door openings. They had planned that they would appear as though dust had been disturbed from the initial opening movement.

At that moment; Captain smiley, caused a commotion to draw attention away from the door, but now as they resumed their posture, the pirates could plainly see that only Rocco and Tuwa stood between the two sets of doors as they closed the outer, while opening the inner.

Rocco entered with his friend and slowly noted where Captain Smiley was in a central position still secured, while at the same time nonchalantly searching for the explosives. It seemed that these people had a reasonable idea of how to set up and contain the area.

The leader stood at the far end of the room and Rocco could make out that he had control of a press button on his waistband.

Rocco spoke to Smiley who had been gagged and asked if he had been mistreated. Smiley shook his head, unable to speak, while Rocco transferred his thoughts asking where the explosives where? Smiley did what he did best but was unsure. He gave what appeared to be a broad grin under the gag. However, he was able to tell Rocco that there was another man in the small room behind them so three of them altogether.

Rocco asked lord Tuwa to start the discussions and to give them everything they asked but only after all the prisoners had been removed.

He was playing their game; the Pirates had no idea of what was happening outside the command centre.

The atmosphere became more relaxed and Tuwa slowly inched a little closer bit by bit toward the leader as they discussed the terms, and the hand over procedure.

Suddenly, within mid sentence came a horrific scream from the room behind them, the leader was caught off guard his arms were suddenly pulled back to be held behind him by the second shadow who slowly materialised. The third Pirate swivelled towards Tuwa raising his weapon to shoot as Rocco's knife entered his neck and he fell dead.

Tuwa quickly grabbed and removed the leader's belt and switch, which had been thoughtfully tied down. Rocco sent him to sleep with a special commando finger hold to the neck. Tuwa acknowledged the movement ` God Rocc, I really should learn that for my future protection, ` they both laughed.

Rocco picked up and examined the belt. It would seem that the leader had grown tired of holding the switch in the depressed position for so many hours; he had not expected such a long takeover and had taped it down. `What luck, ` he exclaimed ` I had not thought they would be so stupid, ` and gave an amazing grin?
He turned to his friends, ` well; we have done well thanks to our new friends. ` Ix-Chel and her companion had now regained their human form and although they did not speak their copied facial expressions, said it all.
Lord Tuwa; only recently aware of the existing life form on his planet, watched in startled disbelief to see Rocco hugging one tall Mayan in particular and drawing the other closer to him for the start of a very special relationship. This he thought would be a very special day to remember.

Captain Smiley Spansetgar, now released from his bonds joined the huddle of Rocco's group celebrations, while the dangers of the explosives, were de-activated and removed. Captain Smiley's first orders were, ` please open the doors, and get that man searched, chained and taken to the security-holding cell. `
With this, suddenly the strained atmosphere changed to joy as the doors opened revealing the supporting team- players patiently waiting with some trepidation; now at last, they could see what was happening inside the Command centre and simultaneously started to clap and cheer the heroes of the day.

Appi was the first to rush in; she had ignored the orders of safety and wanted to be with her man whatever the outcome. She found Tuwa and Rocco standing very close together, still holding hands like brothers brought together for the first time after years of separation.

 They walked across the room unable to release each other, ` I thought we were done for when he raised that firearm ` Tuwa paused in thought. `You Sir astound me.   What a throw, so perfect; if it had missed, I can't bear to think about it.  We would certainly all be dead. `

Appi kissed them both on the cheek then hugged and wound herself around her man while telepathically suggesting to him what they were going to do as soon as they can get away.

Rocco introduced his two new friends to Appi, who was unaware as to their real identities, that would come later,

However, for now Rocco painfully explained that they all must leave and return to the Invistor star. He explained that the rest of the family were waiting anxiously there and as he explained to Tuwa, his friends and family were not only very hungry but, he had the headache of the century and just had to get to the medical wing and have nurse chat-a-lot stitch up his wound. He laughed.   ` Alcohol lots of alcohol. We all deserve a much wanted mad party, `   and with a knowing wink and smirk, he begins to sing for the first time, since leaving Earth with Appi. Suddenly Rocco surprises everyone by starting a conga line with Ix-Chel at the head, and Elder behind him all hip hopping and dancing their way to the shuttlecraft bays where everyone is treated to alcoholic drinks as they embark onto each craft. A slightly inebriated Rocco shouts. ` `How can we not enjoy ourselves, now we are all together surrounded by our friends? ` He appears to be a little merry as he shows Tuwa, Sawston and Awotz, their wives and all the guests how to do the Paul Jones dance, and typically Rocco, managed it all in the back area of the shuttle craft while singing, ` we are going to party. `

He glances across to the two Shadows and suddenly stops, puts his arms around their shoulders with a broad smile. ` You two, ` He starts. ` You two have shown great courage, I shall never forget. `

Rocco seemed to slur a little as he went on, ` this must never be forgotten, we will all sit together by the evening fires, telling and re-telling what happened this day. I shall neeeev.......... ` Captain Rocco slid slowly to the floor and everyone laughed but on arrival aboard the Star, Nurse Chat-a-lot confirmed that his head wound was more serious than first thought and asked for assistance to carry him to the surgery. Ix-Chel without hesitation picked him up as if a small child and carried him close to her breast all the way to the emergency section of the surgery.

It was several days later, when the hero of The Aparsuent returned to take his place with the other assembled residents of Mayan at the designated court house.

Chapter Eight

The Jurors that had been selected were from the home planet, and the planet Freedom to make a legal, diverse and fair selection. It was going to be a quiet trial, as the assembled prisoners and their leader stood in ignominy chained together in the courtroom. They could hardly claim to be not guilty since they had all been captured by the community.

In their favour was the fact that only bruises and humiliation had occurred from their attack. However, in the retaking of the ship there were six deaths, which incensed the friends and relatives of the bloodthirsty pirates and conspirators who had gathered in force to frighten the judge and jurors.

In the minds of the desperate families, they thought that despite the wickedness of the assembled kin, they would be able to threaten and persuade the ignorant peasants of this planet into a lesser sentence, perhaps even admonish the charge of piracy to miss conduct.

However, piracy was a very serious charge that at most held the death penalty and perhaps life in prison for those judged to be not so dangerous.

However, the crux was that the planet Mayan did not have a facility big enough to hold so many for such a long time.

For the knowledgeable citizens of Mayan, it soon became apparent that they had never had such high category prisoners on this home planet, only minor crimes occurred and certainly never one that invoked the death penalty.

Now suddenly it begged the question, ` what would they do with all these people? ` One senior advocate stated.

` We do not have the facilities to hold, feed and guard one person let alone a whole gang of murdering pirates for life, whatever that may be judged to be. `

Prior to the trail, a long-winded discussion had taken place with senior members of the community. They had drawn up an agreement not to execute the leader but, mistakenly or not, everyone wanted to transfer the whole gang of pirates, to a small, distant, and obscure moon, which being marginally barren had just the necessities for life and would be the perfect answer.

This agreement put to the rest of the community had a much more favourable reception; everyone agreed that despite the prisoner's protestations, it was a far better punishment than incarceration or hanging and someone pointed out, ` a lot cheaper.`

They would make their way like the great pioneers of the past, learning to hunt, fish and build homesteads.

It was not known, if any indigenous inhabitants occupied the chosen moon so, the only concession the court would allow for them, was female volunteers who really wanted to accompany them.

So, it was settled, (or, so they thought) until fear again raised its ugly head. Someone shouted from the prisoner's bench; ` we'll be back; we will be back to get you chicken heads and next time, no quarter will be given, you will all die. ` The community's fears were justified. Everyone had thought about it, but said nothing.

The surrounding planets were full of colonists who could interfere, perhaps even the original contractors who were thought to be members of the Conglomerate of planets.

Now from this nervous distress of what might be, came a new idea that startled the meeting. It actually developed from Lord Tuwa's wife Tepintri. She had listened to the discussions with great interest. Nobody could get away from the fact that whatever they do, wherever they decide to take the prisoners, there will always be that fear in the back of their minds, that every local planet had the availability of space travel.

It was one of those moments when everyone was arguing and waving their hands; when Tepintri, sighed almost indistinctly, and uttered under her breath ` not if they are designated to the past! `

Tuwa sat bolt upright, amazingly amongst all that fuss, he had heard her sigh and immediately understood what she had said. Yet, it had come as a whisper among the chaos.

` Yes. ` He shouted. ` We will go into the past. `

Silence descended into the room. ` My friend Captain Rocco managed it.  I think we must consult his opinion. `

The Invistor Star was away visiting the newly discovered planet of Shambhala, an ancient name from Moofee history and more to the point thought to be an appropriate choice by the Lady Appisommati, Adberry. Appi's mother.

She had thought it up during the Star's orbit around the planet and indicated that if it were uninhabited, the name Shambhala would be a perfect name for the Moofee colonists of the future. The whole family, including nurse chat-a-lot, their new friends Ix-Chel and Elder; Who was now permanently named, because everyone thought the name Elder suited his calm wisdom and more to the point, Captain Rocco liked the name. Elder, who deemed his name portrayed a position of trust seemingly enjoying his new status of unity with people that had accepted his friendship.

The two Shadows, had assumed a roll of protectors, no one had asked them and to be honest Rocco rather liked the idea. The Shadows as the name infers, wanted to follow him everywhere and would do so anyway, no matter what he said. It was a form of hero worship.

Under any other circumstance, it could be a little fatiguing but, the science department had made a small device, that could be strapped onto the wrist making conversation now possible, by translating the speech patterns between both parties.

On this glorious day, they had all ventured down by shuttlecraft to enjoy hopefully, the peace and tranquillity of the planet. Rocco had not quite recovered from his head wound and Appi thought that they should spend some time together before the follow up excursion back to the city of Ixi-kore.
This new planet was indeed beautiful and appeared to have everything except inhabitants. It had caused some speculation as they wandered around studying the views and distant sea line.
There seemed very little life within the rocky soil perhaps because of the lack of water.
Nurse Chat-a-lot took charge of April and kept a keen visual watch at everything she did while Appi and her parents went for a slow walk accompanied by Elder who listened intently but said nothing.
Rocco had spotted some interesting flora and discovered that some had shrivelled fruit resembling grapes. It was difficult to tell if the broken stems were a progression from a wild vine or not, until further along, some more lay shrivelled and neglected not exactly in great numbers nor together but certainly in a line.
He wondered about the possibilities and spoke aloud, `could there have been some enterprise once on this planet ` Ix-Chel just looked at him bemused, that this great man was interested in some mouldy old fruit.

`Do you think this is something special? ` She enquired through the hand device. He stood now, saying `they should walk a bit further to see if there were any more. `

Rocco reached another spot further along and called, ` Hey Ix-Chel, come and see, there are some more vines and they are defiantly in a straight line, ` he said delightedly. `This means that they were deliberately planted here in the past. `

Ix-Chel looked alarmed, `but this planet is supposed to be unoccupied, isn't it?

`Mmm, well it probably is now but let's keep alert. `

He called Appi by telepath, not wanting to alarm anyone and asked her to return.

Then as he reached the end of the line of old stumps, he noticed that a dead shrub hid an opening between two large rock formations. It was very narrow and would just allow one slim person to slide through at a time, could be a dwelling, he thought.

Rocco's imagination started to suggest that this could lead to a cave, perhaps even to a more ancient place of interest.

He wanted to enter and called Appi again, he told her to hurry. He was excited, and could hardly wait to show them what he had found.

Appi arrived breathless, his call had made her think of an emergency and then seeing that it was nothing, started to scold him. However, her father was most interested in the vines and being a knowledgeable man with a qualified experience of wine production, he studied the limp dying stems while Appi laughed and joked with her mother about men and their obsession with alcohol.

These two are as alike as peas and put them together anywhere near wine production, where they seem to go into a frenzy especially when they find a pure fermentation from an old barrel.

` Don't knock what you don't understand my dear, ` retorted her father. Rocco nodded and the two men high fived.
` Oh they are incorrigible ` her mother scooped up April and continued. ` Just ignore them daughter. `

Duvan and Rocc now followed the line of distressed vines to the opening and investigated the possible cave entrance while discussing the possibility of previous occupants, when Ix-Chel seemed to be very interested in something just inside the opening. She scented something and started to slide in. Rocco was right behind her and after a struggle between the two shafts of rock for quite a distance; he emerged onto a narrow ledge where Ix-Chel was waiting.
There they contemplated the zigzag pathway going straight down the cliff face into a valley that appeared to be enclosed on all sides by mountains making it into a microclimate where nature had painted everything in brilliant Technicolor for as far as they could see.
The valley stretched far beyond Rocco's line of sight. He could just make out white misty clouds of hydro energy produced by a magnificent fall of water that escalated outwards into a fantastic rainbow, arcing across the whole of the valley.
They looked at each other and Rocco could see tears beginning to form in the corners of her eyes.
She wiped them on his shirtsleeve and whispered.
` I can smell them! ` He looked quizzedly at her.
` I can smell my people Rocc. They were here, We must arrange somehow to go down!`
'But; Ix-Chel. ` He exclaimed, not today for my sake, it is too far down, a sheer drop; if you slip that will be the end. We will talk about it back on the Star and arrange with Tuwa to use his transporter. That, with any luck will put us directly into the centre of any habitable area down below.

I cannot believe that this is so green and full of life. What beauty, it's a paradise hidden away.

 It had taken some time for them to assess the valley, they could not pull themselves away until a voice called from behind, and Appi joined them. She was stunned, ` this cannot be true Rocc. Is it what they call on Earth, a mirage? Why, I have never seen such beauty, do you think there is some way we can get down there safely?
Look at that rainbow! Rocco we must go. ` We will my love perhaps tomorrow with Tuwa. We will go! But, this time, we give a warning before we start to enter the area. Just in case, there are life forms. `
Appi took Ix-Chel's hand. ` Do you think anyone is down there? ` She nodded her head `I can smell my people and It is possible that some may be. Perhaps a colony but the scent is quite old in this passageway. `
Rocco interrupted, ` we will know tomorrow, I will ask Tuwa to accompany us. We can use his transporter. `

Appi could not wait to tell her parents what they had discovered. Her father wanted to go and see for himself but he could not fit his belly into the crevice.
`Never mind father. ` Appi expanded on what they had seen and assured him that they would be making a visit to the area the very next day from a different direction. She did not want to elaborate, thinking it would be much better to just do it and explain afterwards the intricacies of molecular transfer.
The family and guests spent an exhausting afternoon and evening until the shuttle returned. It had been quite a day even little April had fallen asleep with her grandmother on the return trip.

Later after everyone had rested and changed from the outing, they all met in the visitors lounge for drinks and an evening meal. Rocco received a request from Tuwa to join them when the Ja'Way came along side. As friends Rocco and Tuwa were always pleased to join any lounge party and with their exuberance on expanding their individual stories it was difficult to part them once the yarns had began.

However, on this day the betting was to guess, which one would break a blood vessel, to be first to impart the fantastic news of the day. It went from one exploding his news to the other and ended with both of them actually trying to out excite the other, by both speaking at the same time.

Thank God, for Appi and Tepintri who together managed to get control and calm the situation? Appi and Rocco were intrigued and with further questioning, Tuwa with Tepintri's help related exactly what had happened at the court and they were all very excited until Tuwa imparted the news that he and the court wanted to take the prisoners away from the present time and deliver them into the past.

Rocco could feel a deep depression coming over him. He had seen little except work and danger since they had left Earth. This would mean more worry and anxiety. `Why don't we just dump the whole lot into a black hole? ` He asked. ` I can't believe that after what they tried to do, we, or anyone else for that matter, wants to get involved. ` He smiled a knowing smile. ` Maybe it's because I am tired, but all of a sudden I have not only the return to the city of Shadows to negotiate  a peace deal but also an  adventure on the new planet that  I really want to do and now the bloody Pirates who are of no consequence.  I have hardly seen my family. `

Appi looked surprised at his outburst; this was not like Rocco at all. Then she noticed his head was bleeding again near the recent stitches that had somehow not completely healed.

They got him to sit down while nurse chat-a-lot was called to check him over. She declared that `Captain Dear had broken a stitch , possibly from the different atmospheric pressure on the journey down  to the planet, she thought that he could have a slight  concussion, ` nurse then insisted he be taken to the infirmary for head examination in case of any internal bleeding that may cause a blood clot on the brain.
The previous blow to the head had done more damage than they had supposed.
Suddenly Ix-Chel became aware of the urgency and her whole body again changed into the tall muscular Mayan that the team had anxiously met on the planet below.
 She lifted his body, holding him really close to her chest, raising her Captain up as though he weighed nothing in her arms and followed Nurse Chat-a-lot, who now insisted the Captain return to the specialist surgery where he was gently laid on the operating table, so that the computer Doctor and mechanical surgeon could scan and make tests.
Leaving the surgery, Ix-Chel then returned to normal and embraced Appi as they joined all the others outside.

Ix-Chel felt responsible for his condition. It was her absolute guarantee for his safety that persuaded him to go down for the missing child and regrettably it was one of her people that struck the vicious blow that should have killed him.
Her remorse for failing to see the blow coming brought her to tears and great regret as she sat with all the family and friends silently in deep thought. It would be disastrous if anything happened to Rocco.
 He must have been in great pain and said nothing. He was their leader and closest friend and they all loved him.
As the night progressed, the mechanics of the computer surgeon performed a minor operation on the Captain sealing a bleeding blood vessel within his cranium whilst drawing out the pool of excess blood using new technology that also

remodelled the small intrusion, neatly sealing and covering it within his own hairline.

Rocco slept long and deep for the first time that week. Nurse Chat-a-lot stayed at his bedside within the operating theatre watching throughout the night, until all the indications showed that the emergency had passed.

He was then taken to the recovery ward nearby where everyone gathered around his bed like an audience expecting him to perhaps, perform some amazing trick or theatrical turn.

However, it was the noise, that concerned him and brought about an early awakening, no one seemed overly worried that he was trying to sleep. He strained to sit up and enquired if anyone had died?

They all laughed nervously, more from relief rather than amusement. The room returned to life, making his desperate need for facilities an embarrassment as a second nurse Drone appeared with bedpan that initiated a room clearance.

The rest of the day, it was visitors and sleeping until Appi joined him for the night. She had replicated their first night together on the Star after he had been electrocuted by the security Drone. It was strange but wonderful as Appi pushed together the two single beds, curled up with him and slept.

When Rocco awoke, it was to the sounds of laughter. He was fully refreshed after a sonic shower and managed to make his own way to join everyone in the lounge.

Cheers acknowledged his arrival, as he ordered a hearty brunch. He had unwittingly overslept (he thought) but astounded to find that he had actually missed two whole days. No wonder he was so hungry.

The rest of the day was quiet and relaxing until Tuwa returned from Mayan and brought up the business in hand. He maintained that it was urgent to dispatch the prisoners, who were now causing trouble and some of the guards had been bribed. A decision had to be taken to speed up justice by removing them the next day.

Rocco agreed. He had missed his friends Ix-Chel and Elder; they had, he was informed, taken the initiative and a new supply of their special ambrosia down to the City of Ixi-kore. They should have returned by now. This deeply disturbed him and his plans.

It had been Rocco's intentions to take the two Shadows with him on this trip into the past. After which he had hoped that they would eventually become part of his crew.

Appi had intercepted his thoughts and with a tender caress to his ear, she ordered an interpreter Drone with skills of the Ixi-kore dialect to be sent it down to collect them via Tuwa's transporter on the Ja'Way.

Chapter Nine

After lunch, there was still no news from the main City but Tuwa had made another disturbing and urgent call to Rocco's communications section on the Star. `The prisoners had escaped. ` He could not believe it. `Oh Bloody great` shouted Rocco. `Is there no one that can trusted?
 He ordered the star to return immediately to Mayan and take up a close position with the Ja'Way. Rocco chose a team that included some of his guests, which also included Sawston and transferred across to the Ja'Way to teleport down to meet Tuwa and Awotz. His friend was distraught ` thank god you have come. The prisoners have escaped and taken arms from the guards. ` Rocco interceded ` have they left the planet? ` He asked.
Tuwa sat down heavily, putting his head in his hands.
`No worse than that, they have taken hostages and gone down to the city below. `
Rocco immediately sent a telepathic message to the Star and tried to contact the Drone that had gone to fetch Ix-Chel and Elder.
The main thing, he thought, is that these people do not get their hands on the transporter rings carried by the Drone. Under these potentially dangerous circumstances, he ordered that the Drone must destroy itself with the rings before capture. He turned and looked at Tuwa. `After we have transferred down it might be wise to close down the transporter section, just in case and I think it's a good idea to move the Ja'Way and the Star nearer to the Aparsuent flag ship. ` Tuwa agreed. `We should go down now, before they kill everyone and take over the city.

Rocco and Tuwa's parties arrived near the spot where Rocco had been injured, he nearly cried when he saw the vandalism that had been done to the Statue. They had ripped off chunks of gold and an arm that must have taken six men to carry. Solid gold has beautiful properties but the weight, `that should slow them down a bit, ` he thought.

The whole area was strewn with debris and several creatures had been killed although it seemed that the pirates had moved on and that would give them time to form a plan while they waited for contact from the Drone.

Rocco ordered the men to make a back-to-back circle so that they could not be surprised then tried to make contact himself but with what he saw around him it looked hopeless, the pirates had cleaned out that whole area, they seemed so confident that they didn't even leave a rear guard.

Around him, lay some old weapons discarded not perhaps of their age but they had acquired better. No wonder they were confident, perhaps they had found more advanced hand weapons in the city and could match the firepower of the Ja'Way.

Rocco relayed his thoughts to Tuwa who looked even more concerned. ` I should have listened to you; these animals are not fit to walk this planet. I have made a grave mistake. Rocco we must win at all costs they must not be allowed to reach the surface again. `

Tuwa stopped talking and Rocco ordered the team to move quickly forward. The group made and retained a circular shape so that they could cover their advance. This they maintained until they reached the other side of the square where a pirate was spotted in a window, but eliminated by a single shot from an unknown source.

As they squatted each covering the other, Rocco received a message from his Drone. ` Captain, friend Elder is covering your advance. ` `Thank god for the Drone and his friends, he thought. `

The Drone continued ` The pirates have split their forces into two parties. They are aware that you have arrived and one party is approaching the Seagate exit, looking to find a working craft with weapons. `

How do you know this? Have you been taken? ` Rocco telepathed .

` No Captain, we are hidden in an obsolete tower that overlooks the whole city. The prisoners are regrouping with weapons they have found. I have also been assured, by friend Elder, who had changed and joined them for a while but, Elder says the pirates are in for a shock.

It appears that only half of that group are now human they are being quietly disposed of and replaced by Shadows.

Captain you should know that the second group have circled behind you, but don't worry they are about to meet a lot of beautiful ladies, Elder says that you will understand their fate. ` Rocco grinned from ear to ear. ` Ahaa , femme-fatale, what a way to go. ` He turns to his group. `Gentlemen, in a little while, the city will be ours. On no account must anything be taken and try not to kill anyone because things are not what they seem. Our main objective now is to secure all the exits and take possession of the Star ships and shuttlecraft outside the dome. `

Tuwa now fully briefed at what was happening and asked about the remaining prisoners? Rocco held nothing back. `

As to the Prisoners, No one is to leave here alive. ` This brought a gasp, `That is the law. `Rocco concluded, `I do not wish to do this again, I think we must follow the law: Piracy is punishable by death. `

At this point, the assembled crew with Lord Tuwa were confronted by a party of Mayan women and girls, led by a striking beauty that everyone recognised and made Lord Tuwa's eyes nearly pop out of their sockets.

That was bad enough, but when Rocco was grabbed; and embraced nearly to the floor by the voluptuous Tepintri, it was the last straw. Rocco laughed and hugged her unrestrictedly as Tuwa became enraged to the point of drawing his gun.

He stood in dumb fold disbelief, his hands shaking.

Then the couple released themselves and revealed Rocco's friend Ix-Chel now growing in size, glaring at him and his gun while letting out a scream that could curdle any living matter.

` For God's sake, Tuwa put that bloody gun away. These people are our friends and future allies. Remember, I did warn you that nothing is, as it seems. `

Rocco went to his friend to calm his obvious anger and embarrassment. They sat together on the steps where Rocco, had been attacked and talked of all the things, that had happened.

As the gathering teams, from the surface grew in numbers, Rocco and Tuwa, made inquiries about the Pirate leader.

This, was the man that they most desperately wanted. Some rumours had started, that a few members thought he was definitely dead but there was no evidence to support the claim. Then, Elder reminded Rocco that a small party of Pirates had gone ahead of the main group and it became apparent that he may have slipped out of the city taking one of the smaller craft and reaching the surface.

This could be disastrous if it managed to enter one of the Star ships. The nearest was the Ja'Way and it had access to everything but, more to the point it especially controlled the transporter.

Rocco took the decision to leave the planet and return to the Ja'Way where he found only a skeleton crew manning the ship. The vital areas were unattended. His arrival caused some controversy; they had not expected anyone to return for some time and panicked when such a high authority suddenly materialised.

Rocco had a reputation of fairness, but they had seen his other side. He could kill anyone that crossed him. Now they panicked, he had caught them all in the galley drinking and he was angry. Rocco voiced his thoughts by shouting about their fellow shipmates, who were risking their lives below while they had no thoughts for anything else but themselves. He could not believe that there was no one stationed on the bridge and it was obvious that for this reason, no one had seen any craft leaving the planet.

On the related news of what had happened, the crew scrambled into action as Rocco continued to reprimanded them; he then went on to explain that there was a strong possibility that while they were all enjoying themselves the leader had escaped from the main confrontation and may have found a working shuttlecraft.

 He went on. ` With this craft they could  come straight up to the surface and confront the nearest Warship; That's you. `
He shouted, `you knob head imbeciles.  Let's hope they have used their intelligence and travelled underwater to the other side of the planet. `

With these thoughts, Rocco told the crew that they should now move a far distance away from the planet and form a triangle with the Star and the Aparsuent.

He then left the ship accompanied by his two guardians to rejoin the Invistor Star.

It would take some while for the shuttlecraft to travel across to the Star and Captain Rocco, had started to cool down somewhat.

 His thoughts turned to what had happened and he re-considered what he had said earlier to the crew and suddenly laughed aloud to everyone's amusement. ` They would have no idea what a knob head was, ` and he continued laughing to himself.

By the time the little shuttlecraft reached the Star, his mood was more amenable. He always found arrivals a relief and much more enjoyable especially as he and Captain Appi embraced and kissed as he briefly explained the situation to her and Smiley Spansetgar. They then arranged the deployment of the three ships into a triangular position giving them complete all round vision of the entire area.
In this way, he could combine and triangulate the three ships detectors to cover and pick up any movement above and below the oceanic surface of the planet Mayan.
This was a clever move and it didn't take long before a message arrived from the Ja'Way that two small objects had left the planet on the far side, just as Rocco had predicted. The only problem now was whether the second craft was in pursuit or part of the pirate's crew of cutthroats.
`This man is certainly devious, ` he spoke aloud. ` Is it possible that both craft are decoys? ` Then he made up his mind, ` we will use tractor beams and grab them both. `
It was simple enough, except as they approached to connect the beams the second ship unexpectedly exploded with such force that the Invistor Star was physically thrown aside, and sped uncontrollably backwards a great distance allowing the first craft to escape .

Rocco could not pursue, he and his crew struggled to slow down the Invistor Star while trying to recover enough control to turn the ship around back towards Mayan.
He was in fact so busy that he forgot about Captain Smiley until they heard a terrific boom on the horizon, leaving a

great black cloud of smoke that vanished just as fast as the time it had taken for the sound to reach them.

Now came panic, as his thoughts conjured up the possibilities of what had happened.

Had the Aparsuent, been attacked? What had caused such a big explosion? His answers came swiftly as Smiley spoke to them by Telepathy. The shuttlecraft had turned and attacked the Aparsuent head on and had been destroyed.

Rocco wondered about the action, why had the Pirates attacked. They knew they could not defeat a battle ship.

In his mind, he was trying to make sense of their action.

`What would I do? ` his thoughts raced and he ordered the Star to join the Ja'Way and surround the Aparsuent immediately.

His orders were that they would board Captain Spansetgar's ship and take control.

Sawston transferred back onto the Ja'Way and took control, while Captain Tuwa was clearing up the mess in the City below.

He said nothing but thought Rocco had gone mad, `why ` he thought, `what could be the reason to now suddenly dash back and forcibly board this ship again? ` But, he followed his instructions to the letter.

Four teams transferred across to the Aparsuent, two by transporter into the lower crew's quarters on both sides of the ship, the third one into the command centre where the Captain, if found, could control the search and the ship, while Rocco and his team would enter at the rear by shuttlecraft, landing in the service bay.

Rocco's first action on arrival was to inform Captain Smiley, what they were doing. He now apologised and requested that a full scan be performed on the outside area for any escape pods. Smiley took it all in his stride and Rocco could see by his facial expressions that Captain Smiley was somewhat bemused and did not understand what the reasons were for all these precautions.

Rocco sat him down and went on to clarify the importance of why the Aparsuent would be completely searched for intruders. `You see, my friend, they may have transferred over when the explosion occurred. `

It was a tricky situation. If the pirates had learnt the secrets of the transporter and used the shuttlecraft as decoys, they may have transferred aboard. Otherwise where had they gone? Why did they change course and attack the Aparsuent? No survival pods have been detected elsewhere. Could it be a double bluff!

Were they still on the planet and planning to reappear when the dust had settled?

Mayan was one of the biggest planets of un-tapped resources in that galaxy and compatible with the planet Freedom. The newly discovered underground city, a vast unexplored metropolis of vast riches, judging by the golden statue it would certainly inspire the fever for great wealth and the sort of people they were fighting.

He looked directly at Smiley. 'They could hide anywhere in there for years. `

This was the first time that Rocco had seen Captain Smiley in serious thought and the long silence was broken by a messenger. ` Lord Tuwa's compliments if the situation is now resolved could he have his shuttle back. ` Rocco left the room to reply directly via the communications section. He solemnly gave Tuwa the known facts then followed with his thoughts about the possibilities of the leader being still in the city but perhaps aboard one of the three remaining Battleships.

`This is bad` Tuwa growled ` I do not have enough people to cover the fleet as well as the land. I only hope you are wrong. ` He paused. `If only we could get aboard them and disconnect something.

Rocco could not think of any other way, except entering each ship in turn by transporter and monotonously going through each nook and crevice throughout each Star ship. It would take weeks and time is of the essence.

` Ill go over to the Ja'Way ` he called ` I need to speak to Pakal. `   As he turned Appi arrived with little April in her arms. The child stretched its arms towards him and bubbled sounds of pleasure as he leaned forward to hold her. He caress her face with multiple baby kisses and thoughts that made him wish they were alone, just the three of them enjoying a normal happy day.

They walked slowly down the corridor towards the visitor's lounge where Ix-Chel and Elder joined them just as Tepintri suddenly appeared in a puff of smoke with Appi's parents. She looked amazing in a tight fitting garment that hid a new tiny bulge.

He did not need to close his eyes to remember that night and as the women greeted with hugs and kisses, Rocco sneaked a quick glance at Ix-Chel, who was smiling directly at him which caused a hot flush to touch his cheek and a shiver that run down the whole length of his spine.

Chapter Ten

Time was not his friend this day, as he prepared to return to the Ja'Way. He looked at Appi and conveyed a sorry status, explaining that he had to go and asked her to contact Smiley to arrange the ships triangle position as before.
This time his arrival on the Ja'Way, everything was in order as he made his way directly to the secret room in the Captains quarters. His faithful companions followed taking a great interest in the security screens. They were amazed that they could watch everything within the whole ship. Ix-Chel screeched her delight but froze with shock when Pakal suddenly appeared with his deep voiced ` by your command. `

Rocco laughed. ` Pakal` he started, `I need your expertise.`
 Pakal answered; in his formidable way; `by your command Captain Rocco` and waited.
It was rather a lot to say as Rocco explain the whole situation. He like Tuwa still had not grasped the subtleties that this was a machine run by a computer and needed no explanations but felt better for it, as he finished with a question. `Pakal, can you communicate with the guardians of the fleet? `
There came now a long eerie silence that followed suddenly six flickering security screens that lit up.
Both shadows suddenly became aggressive screeching and bearing their teeth as each screen beheld the image of Pakal. The screens stared at him and in unison, boomed out, `by your command. `
Rocco nearly jumped for joy as the original Pakal explained about a machine code communication that allowed all interface commands to be shared by the whole fleet.

`Gentlemen, Guardians of the fleet, ` he started as though on a platform addressing his constituents in an election.

` Lord Tuwa and I request instructions on confining the unmanned fleet in its present position or dock. We request that no access be given to any ship or any of their facilities. Allow nothing.

No movement may be made away, from their present positions and

 no use of any transporters. Do you have the control to affect these orders? `

The response was immediate. ` Yes Captain Lord, by your command `

Rocco breathed a deep sigh of relief ` these orders do not apply to the Ja'Way.

We are looking for a group of hostile alien humans that have killed many Mayans and it is possible that they may have taken refuge or be hiding within the fleet. Do you have any sense of unauthorised movement within your ships?   Again, the answer was a swift no except for one screen, ` Captain Lord, I find that there are some alterations within the engineering section. An attempt to make start up has been made, without success. `

Rocco immediately commanded; ` you will stop all life giving facilities. Any Oxygen available must be removed. Ventilate the entire ship then, pump in carbon monoxide gas to all areas. ` He paused for thought, ` who are you, what ship are you?

`Captain Lord, I am Pakal of the Chan -Way (Sky Spirit) . By your command; it is done. `

`Thank you Pakal, I wish to be address as Captain Rocco and I would like Pakal of the Ja'Way to update you all on the current present day situation and upgrade your computers with the new knowledge and translations in readiness for your new crews.

In the event that any Star ship of the fleet is boarded, contact must be made immediately to me or Captain Commander Lord Tuwa of Mayan.

`By Your Command, Captain Rocco; 'they all chorused.

At that Rocco and friends turned to leave and found Sawston patiently waiting in the corridor. ` Hello my friend ` Rocco chipped, are we in position to view the whole planet. `   ` Yes Captain. `

The following day relaxed from his labours and in the knowledge that the despots and their leader (hopefully) had at last been eliminated.

They would never be completely sure until they entered the Sky Spirit and with this always-in mind, he had maintained a high alert and suggested the same for the Ja'Way and the Aparsuent with a continuous watch for anything leaving the planet.

Rocco and his companions Ix and Elder took a shuttlecraft down to the planet Mayan, to collect his friend Tuwa and the remaining crews.

Their arrival was hardly noticed and Rocco could see party celebrations as they approached the landing site. His friend Tuwa was standing in the middle of a crowd, with a glass in his hand raising it to the crew that cheered each time he raised the glass. Rocco watched with amusement from a distance until the general back slapping and jollities had ended then the two friends came together and drew Awotz closer to them to be able to hear above the noise. ` Friends ` Rocco began, `I think we have a lot more problems than we ever imagined. We are now, ` he corrected himself, ` well we soon will be, the largest battle force in the galaxy. ` He studied Tuwa's face. ` Tuwa, do you remember the discussions that we had on the beach, that night we had set up the tents on planet Freedom? ` Tuwa nods his head and winks as he turns to face Awotz with the gravest of expressions. I hope you will understand what I have to say Awotz. You, have proved yourself to be; outstanding in battle and as a senior member of my crew, our friendship is unrivalled. Nevertheless, everything has to change.

We are building a great force and I regret that I have to let you go from my crew. You see, with the addition of the three battleships Sawston, we will need a crew to train, command, and help us maintain the peace. ` A long pause of silent regret followed.

This was an unexpected major disappointment for a man that had given his all, he believed what they had told him from the very beginning and despite this set back he respected their decision especially Rocco who was now smiling at him as Tuwa continued. ` I cannot have you in my crew because you are to be Captain on a new Star ship.    ` What do you think Captain Awotz? `

This was pure shock for Awotz. They could see the tears welling up in his eyes. ` My Captain he stammered this is the greatest honour. `

Rocco and Tuwa grasped Awotz hands and both slapped his shoulders. We are proud to be at last able to offer all those things associated with true loyalty and a special friendship that binds us together. Now we must go to the Ja'Way, I would like a Captains meeting and see if Captain Sawston can open some of that special Mayan brandy. ` They all laugh as they turn towards the waiting Drones and Rocco's guardians who follow closely as they make their way to the shuttle pick up point.

` Did you bring my shuttle back Captain ` He gently elbowed Rocco in the ribs and quickly remembered the Drones.   ` Rocco, when are you going to tell these tin cans I am a bloody friend? `

This caused another roar of laughter with Tuwa using colloquial terms he'd picked up from close company. It didn't quite fit with the character of the man or the place .

`Captain Tuwa; ` he stifles another chuckle,   ` you know, I cannot tell a lie. ` This brought profound silence. Rocco held his straight face then slowly bursting out with `Appi and I have decided to adopt you and Tepintri which makes you family and an Uncle to boot. `

Tuwa smiles, `This is a great honour` but, seems perplexed at the words to-boot?

` What does this mean? ` He stammers; `Does this mean I get kicked whenever I visit? `

`No, no Tuwa it's an expression, it means as well and little April is already calling you Unc. Well it sounds something like that. `

The banter went on between the whole group, even Ix-Chel managed to screech something that Rocco translated as, ` we would like to be family as well` and chuckled in a strange way, that brought everyone to their knees with laughter, just as the shuttle entered and landed in the service bay.

At this point Captain Rocco stating the obvious as usual, went on to calm the excitement. `I believe we are here gentlemen and lady, as he smiled at Ix-Chel. Tuwa walked forward as the shuttlecraft doors began to open to the sound of music that blasted their arrival. The whole crew had assembled and the Mayan National Anthem echoed throughout the service bay.

As Tuwa exited the craft, he paused at the door holding his hand reverently over his heart until the music stopped.

 The gathered crew and friends cheered and cheered until Tuwa raised his hands and joined with the others that had assembled to the side of the craft behind a Dias that had been especially erected.

That made, Lord Captain Tuwa completely in his preferred element as he climbed the steps to address the assembled crew and dignities.

Clearing his throat and raising his head to the crowd he spotted Sawston; standing insignificantly to the side and rear of the gathering. How typical of him to stand aside, this was not a man to indulge in ceremony, or show off. He had become a respected leader, to all who dwelled on planet Freedom and could be counted on under any circumstance.
Sawston had risked his life for them on several occasions but especially during the fight on the planet below and also with Rocco on the Aparsuent in fact he had stood back to back with all of them since the joining of the planet Freedom.

Now the bay had quietened to a whisper and Tuwa raised his voice to announce how proud he was to be associated with the Captains standing before them.
`However, there is one man missing, a generous man, a man with courage and dignity. A man which; had offered the most precious thing that he had; his life. Now I insist   that he should take his place and join us now. ` He turns and looks across to the crowd. ` Please, join us Captain. ` He paused and pointed. ` Captain Sawston. ` A great cheer went up and a rather embarrassed Sawston joined the group appreciation hug; that then followed with handshakes.

This gave the Mayan – Freedom alliance three war ships and if Rocco stayed with Lord Duvan a total of five ships would be available with one still spare that had to be repaired and cleaned up after removing the dead pirates.
The days that followed were days of joy, peace and planning. Each Captain wanted to assemble his own crew while testing and putting his new ship into perfect working order. This would mean crystal replacements and engineering tests with training for two new crews, which initially did not need too much intervention from Rocco who found himself with time to spare.

The emergencies had subsided and his thoughts sometimes turned to memories of the slow peaceful tranquillity of Earth and the night he met his beloved Appi. His life recently had been gathering more and more momentum, every new day seemed to realise many more new problems, requiring his precious time and neglecting his family. Sometimes during the workload, he would reach a point, especially late at night, when in a state of undress; he would stop and wonder if he were dressing to leave the room or undressing to go to bed. He could just not remember.

 For Rocco, the time seemed to vanished so quickly that he began to wonder if it would ever end for them to continue their original journey.

Perhaps it was the shorter daylight hours or that the planets surrounding Mayan did not allow equal sunlight and depending on the position of the Invistor Star they would, some days be in complete darkness making an unwanted depression and a dreary life.

`When, ` he had thought, ` when would the work and the time equalize?  Would I eventually just disappear in a puff of energised frenzy? `

The answer came to him as usual, from an angelic voice inside his head. ` The only frenzy around here my dearest love is me, ` Rocco immediately relaxed as Appi, invited him to share the space she had lovingly prepared and warmed up especially for him.

She had waited fully prepared, to cover them both with the bedding, and more especially him, with kisses. This was where they had spent to best of many enjoyable hours of intimate fun beneath the covers of darkness.

Chapter Eleven

A few evenings later cocooned in his special den, he felt a sensation that he recognised as a familiar face entered quietly and sat beside him.

 Rocco did not need to speak or look up from his thoughts, he knew instinctively who it was and realised she had been promised a visit to the valley on new planet.

'Hello Ix, ' he started, ' I have not forgotten. I think this is a good time to get away for all of us. I will ask Tuwa to arrange a day off with his transporter on the Ja'Way. ' She purred beside him so close, he could feel her ambiance that urged him to release his tensions but his love for Appi was too strong.

Tuwa was delighted with the idea of a family picnic and despite the imaginative and colourful descriptions he had been given, he did not believe such a place existed on this desolate planet.

However, he now understood the logic that they should consider, there may be a community of some sort in the valley and it would seem like an invasion if everyone suddenly materialised without warning.

Rocco explained that the local populace may even attack or worse shape shift, to defend and attack unseen. Just like, they witnessed at the Aparsuent siege. He went on to suggest that perhaps they should start by just viewing the situation from the mountain pathway then, they could at least try to give warning and even offer goodies that Ix-Chel had suggested to start introductions.

Tuwa nodded in agreement. He, Rocco and a Drone would accompany the two Shadows with a container of the elixir and some pretty things that they hoped would be of some interest.

Rocco was excited for the first time in years at the thought of wine production. Not just to produce the finest vintage but, he had a want to be involved.
In his youth he had helped and studied on a vineyard in France while learning the language and had spent time looking around in Germany marvelling at the efficiency of the Germans and comparing methods, always dreaming that one day he could produce a commodity that could delight just as the ancients had done from the very beginnings of civilisation.

The strange party materialised in an area of rocky desert some distance from the mountain entrance. This gave Rocco the opportunity to point out the remains of the old desiccated vines.
Tuwa was not impressed, but listened politely ` It has not rained for years, maybe centuries, ` he stated, as he kicked the sand surrounds. It was beginning to get hot and the only shade was at the foot of the mountain. Rocco continued ahead pointing out all the items of interest, well the items that he felt of interest that might excite his friend. Nevertheless, Tuwa was picking up the pace to get out of the heat.
Ix-Chel and Elder were already at the entrance of the passageway and quickly disappeared, Rocco followed with Tuwa leaving the Drone (who was to big anyway) at the entrance with instructions to wait, while the two friends made their way to join the Shadows.
Tuwa Gasped at the beauty before him. ` Rocco. ` He went on exhaling a long gasp. ` I owe you an apology; this is beyond anything I imagined. It is exactly as Appi described,

a fantastic hidden paradise, such beauty, encapsulated by this Technicolor arcing across the whole valley. `

`You mean the Rainbow ` Rocco smiled.

Now Suddenly Tuwa was excited. ` We must go, come let's get back and arrange our transporter. ` But Rocco needed more time, to arrange for Ix-Chel to announce them. `Make a message by shouting down into the valley, say, visitors had arrived. ` He was concerned that the waterfall would drown out the message but they should try anyway. She screeched as loud as she could, but there was no reply and after several attempts, Elder volunteered to go down the dangerous winding track.

They all peered nervously over the path edge; the cliff was practically vertical and impossible for any human.   Rocco politely declined the offer; he explained that he was afraid for his friend. If he slipped and fell, he would surely die and even if he succeeded, he may be attacked just as he was, in the city. Do not forget; in this place, you are a complete stranger. Anyway, how would we be able to help you if he got into difficulty?

`Lets return with Tuwa, we will take a chance that they may be more amenable to their own kind. `

On their return to the entrance they found Tuwa pacing up and down; he could not wait to get back and transfer down in to the valley.

Rocco explained to him, that by not, introducing themselves; could start hostilities. ` They may even tear us apart. We need to show we mean no harm but, this time let's take a little protection as well and Tuwa my friend, remember, what their staple diet is and who provides  it? `

Finally, Lord Tuwa had the message; he now understood and suddenly felt a little afraid.

It was then that Elder Screamed and grew taller as he faced towards the mountains. He let out another scream and Ix-Chel joined in.

They all looked toward the valley entrance but could see nothing. Curiosity egged them to move slowly forward as Ix-Chel and Elder went ahead. Suddenly there appeared a head at ground level and then another, followed by a group of strange primates that from this distance away, appeared to be animal. The group gathered outside the mountain entrance. A scruffy pack,; of shaggy, longhaired and wrinkled canine. They reminded him, of some Shar-pei dogs that he had seen in China, their originating birthplace. Their excessive rolls of mangled hair, concealed many layers of excessive flesh that flapped about as they moved doggedly around.

Some stood erect to a height of five feet but, Rocco and Tuwa both knew that they could increase to seven. They were impressive and war like, holding Stone Age weapons in hands just as human as his own while manoeuvring and arranging their feet into a posture of defence. In all senses of the word, they were human in a different form.

It was initially a shock to see them, but not unpleasant as the faces were, in most cases human and very beautiful; especially the females who stood displaying their protruding femininity, oiled and glistening with pride in the sunlight.

As Ix-Chel, Elder and the team moved closer, they could see that the group of warriors were definitely much more human than animal. Perhaps originally they were a species of humans that had become affected by some form of biological deformity, where the mal formation had given this species regenerative power.

If they were the same as the Ixikore Shadows, they had a distinct advantage, that after many generations of evolution which had somehow altered their chromosomes and DNA into a complexity where, self-induction allowed change of shape, following later with pigment that matched whatever shape or form taken.

The greatest of these transformations was into the Shadow, used for invisible defence or complete integration with any species.

Rocco suddenly envisaged himself as a great pioneer or explorer the new Livingstone. Perhaps he had found the source of the Shadows. This was totally unexpected; no one had ever imagined that there existed, on this barren planet, anything but dust. But he had a nagging moment; if these primitives were the source then they were not what they appeared to be. The exterior showed signs of sophistication in taste and knowledge these folks were (according to their dress and manner) certainly not capable of producing a fine bottle of claret. Even their tools were still stone age! And the vine plantation was old but not as old as Stone Age?

The bewildered tribal warriors seemed reluctant to come forward, even though Ix-Chel and Elder were rapidly trying to make conversation. Rocco's translator did not seem to be able to follow what the creatures were saying. Perhaps it was the dialect or more likely a very ancient dialect that suddenly stopped when Elder changed his bodily shape and became the very image of the others as he joined the group.

Almost immediately, the group became a frenzied mass like wasps, turning in circles, pushing and poking. Elder had surprised them and although he couldn't converse in their native language they must have understood some words because they did not immediately kill him. However, he was caught and as an intruder, they were teaching him a lesson. Suddenly, following a painful screeching noise, they all vanished back into the mountain passageway.

Rocco and Ix-Chel rushed forward to intercede just in case Elder had sustained any injury but everyone had completely disappeared just as quickly as they had mysteriously arrived.

Elder had gone! Had he gone willingly, or had he been taken?

Ix-Chel was aggressively angry, she made it quite clear that she wanted to follow but Rocco stopped her. ` I do not want to lose you as well. We will go the other way armed and ready that is if they want a fight. `

Outside, Tuwa was waiting with the Drone just by the opening to the passage way and immediately he saw them he ordered their return back to the Ja'Way.

`This time we will go in strength with extra members of the crew. ` Tuwa continued, ` We should get some recordings of all the dialects from Pakal`s ancient transcripts, ` he stopped, perplexed and looking directly at Rocco. `It could run into thousands of variations and would be extremely difficult to transcribe since their language had not been used for possibly Centuries. `

At this exclamation, Tuwa paused again, with a trance like look on his face. ` A script of basic squeaks and screeches: surely only a computer could decipher this and even then, given the amount of work, can it be done? ` He stops again, ` especially now one of us has been taken; will we have the time? `

Rocco cut in. ` We must make the time; Elder's life may be at stake! ` He suddenly marched off to organise the equipment they would need.

It was turmoil as the crew with designated Drone addressed their priorities. Some assisted the Drone with ancient manuscripts combined with Pakal's downloaded memory banks and then suddenly like magic, everyone was in position and ready to go.

Selected members of the Ja'Way now gathered in the transporter departure area, where Rocco expressed a hope that the groups decent and metamorphosis suddenly out of thin air would stun the local creatures as it had with the city dwellers into thinking they were Gods.

The Invistor Star crew had invested hours of work transferring the latest technology and at last integrated it into the Ja'Way's computer search banks.

With this advanced technical equipment, they were now able to pinpoint exactly where the locals were gathered.

Rocco could plainly see the movements on the planet, as they scurried around and he could see a tall member that appeared to be hanging above the rest of the group.

Rocco thought that Elder must have reverted to his human shape to protect himself.

The tall shape radiated strong colours of red and blue on the inferred screen, as it swayed and violently bobbed up and down.

` I think we had better hurry, ` murmured Rocco.

Tuwa agreed, it was plain to see that the tall figure was in trouble. Lord Tuwa deployed six other men to return with them and as they prepared to depart, he turned to Rocco. ` I like friend Elder. ` An unusual remark from Tuwa; he continued as they entered their transporter cubicles. ` He has proved himself and I have come to change my opinion of these creatures. ` His smile slowly disappeared as the transported took them.

The creatures were caught completely unaware, they were celebrating and physically shocked, at the team's materialisation; giving more than enough time for Rocco to raise his gun and shoot away the leather thongs that held his friend. Elder was hanging vertically from a crudely made line by his wrists, bouncing his body up and down. This had an effect like a vertical accordion squeezing out a moaning sound on every movement upward until he fell to the ground. Rocco tossed his hunting knife across for him to cut and release his ankle ties that were firmly bonded onto stakes deeply imbedded in the soil. He watches while his friend struggles to re-circulate the liquid within the veins of his legs and cannot resist the temptation to   remark smarmily. `Sorry my friend, if we kept you hanging around. We thought that you had joined their gang!` He laughs as Elder screeched something, while returning his knife but Rocco could not mistake the smile of gratitude that crossed Elder's green flushed face as they moved the creatures into a safe position, pinning them closer together against a wall.

Rocco was fascinated by the creatures ability, to move and disappear so quickly and astounded to learn that they could fly. Elder went on to explain that the creatures had grabbed him. `They bundled me to the cliff edge and four of them took an arm and a leg each then, then all jumped together over the edge! ` He elaborates with more detail. `They used their excess flesh somehow, they stretched it outwards to control the air flow,  not exactly like  wings but it allowed them to glide smoothly down as the found a hot air thermal. `
Elder stopped for a minute re- calling his initial fears.
 `The experience of being held and floating uncontrollably, then rapidly descending downwards, horrified me at first but, they do have this remarkable ability to fly. `
Rocco was amazed that they had achieved such a complex ability, ` I wonder how they discovered it, and which, was the first one to fall off the cliff? ` His thoughts made him smile. ` It reminds me of Lemmings, but the comment was completely lost on everyone else, until he explained what Lemmings were and what they occasionally did over cliff edges, without I may add, `he smirked. ` Any; flying equipment. `
This information led to comments and raucous laughter as he added, ` they all died of course. `

Chapter Twelve

The joviality, made him feel secure amongst his friends , in fact secure enough to go for a walk, like the old days into the more denser and un-cleared parts of the valley's overgrown jungle area.
It wasn't long before he was entirely alone and it came into his mind how it all started with the excursion outside the village back on earth. Then he had the experience of the ghostly apparition of Dobbo's grey mare.
However, this time there was no foggy mist and there seemed to be few animals. Certainly no deer, and few birds; he glided skilfully around the vegetation, like a ghost.
Rocco had not forgotten his art and he was really enjoying himself, as he pressed on deeper until he came upon a small clearing that was empty of trees but showed tracks and areas where the grasses had been slightly flattened. So perhaps there was some wild life here after all.
He moved in closer to the central area and saw something move, then again, he saw its head shake within the deep grass; it seemed unaware of his presence.
 The cool breeze was coming towards him so it had not picked up his scent. The animal was quite small and his curiosity drew him closer to see what type of animal it might be.
Suddenly it stood up, its camouflaged exterior was striped, not unlike a tiger, but this was very small and reasonably harmless. It did not run but just stood in the stalking position.
` Oh my God` Rocco exclaimed, this is a cub, please God don't let the mother be close. `

Then it made a high-pitched crying noise, it was obviously alarmed and calling for help as Rocco slowly backed away trying to put as much distance between them as possible and as he reached the protection of the trees he turned and came face to face with the biggest feline animal he had ever seen.

It was far bigger than the man-eaters of Bangladesh in India. These he well remembered, the Bengal tigers that he had seen as an invited member of a hunting expedition.

However, that was strictly controlled, travelling in comfort, safely riding high on the back of an Elephant with his trusted rifle.

This cat was different, not only in size but also displayed an attitude that it was not afraid and who would be if they also had two large canine sabre like teeth, producing a wry like grin.

Rocco knew he was in trouble and all he had was his large hunting knife as the two faced each other.

He knew that he must not run this predator was far fitter than he was. The standoff seemed to last an eternity that dragged on and on as the cries of the cub became longer and stronger.

The mother did not move but stood unblinking, statuesque, waiting and prepared to take him at any false move. When suddenly, he felt something between his legs, it was biting through his costume and purring as it shook its head trying to pull the chewed cloth away.

Rocco stood his ground, and slowly reached down to stroke the cub behind its ears. The little cub left his tattered clothes and started to reciprocate the attention, it purred even louder as it licked his fingers.

Perhaps it was the salt on his hand or perhaps it knew he was going to be for lunch, who knows but Rocco sat down and pretended that the mother was not there.

He was not sure but he gambled that this mother would not attack while he held its baby.

 Rocco averted his eyes away from the mother to the cub as it rolled over into a posture of submission while he continued to tickle its stomach.

This caused the most amazing thing to happen, the mother crawled forward on all fours, then lay beside him like a big pussycat, and allowed him to pet her as well.

`Well my friends ` he whispers, ` I certainly have a way with the girls. ` He laughs and makes his own purring noises as the three enjoyed the encounter and unbelievably they all dozed off while laying comfortably on each other.

At the main camp Lord Tuwa and the two shadows had been trying to get some understanding from their captive creatures as the Drone assessed and accumulated all the sounds it had heard whilst waiting outside the compound. It was assembling those sounds and comparing them with the new, while imputing the ancient information gathered from the Guardian Pakal.

The main warrior creatures had been given some of the new sustenance or ambrosia that Rocco had devised and asked to be manufactured.

 They had seemed to find it palatable as did Elder and Ix-Chel but after the distribution they began to realised that their main responsibility, Captain Rocco, was no longer in the compound.

Dusk was drawing in the darkness, and the area began to explode with an amazing phenomenon of floral light, it made the Ja'Way team transfixed as though drugged. The strange perfumes eluding from the flowers, combined with the psychedelic moving colours, mesmerised all those that watched.

The flowers moved in harmony with the gentle light. It was like silent music as far as the watchers were concerned. Perhaps the pitch was too high or low for humans and only the birds and animals could hear it.

This wonderment of natural beauty was definitely one of Nature's miracles that had surprised everyone except the local populace who ignored it.

These plants and flowers generated their own light and the whole valley began to come alive with beauty that was illuminated from their gathered solar power, drawn during the sunlight hours into the plants own leaf system to power up and allow pollination at night.

Rocco stirred from his sleep as the air chilled around him, he was now alone and the sun slowly departing from the valley, leaving a shadowy blanket slowly extending itself on the already darkened side.

He stared across at the dark forest area, now believing that he was hallucinating, perhaps his thoughts were scrambled as his mind began racing at the marvels now appearing around him . ` I am, either dead and gone to heaven, or someone has spiked my mind with some of those magic mushrooms. `

He spoke aloud while vigorously rubbing his eyes. He could not believe that the foliage around him had begun to twinkle and come alive with colour slowly beginning to get brighter.

` Did I really dream this up? ` His thoughts questioned again his sanity; ` surely not, ` he murmured, ` that would mean my encounter with the Tigers was also a dream. ` He began to touch the flowers, running his fingers along their plant stems and extended both hands, cupping the bulbous flowers gently between them.

The plants responded by donating and covering his hands in a luminous pollen and glowing slime.

The pollen looked and glimmered like the florescent nightsticks. He remembered that children used them for Halloween evenings back on Earth, they displayed like fireflies and words could be written as each stick was moved in the darkness.

Just then, a slight noise caught his attention and Ix-Chel moved out of the darkness to join him.

` You are not alone my Captain, ` she sniffed the air and held his hand as she led him back through the forest. It was unnecessary to be guided, but he enjoyed her company and she loved the prestige of being his guardian and perhaps more, if he so wished.

`Ix-Chel, this is a wonderful place, even the animals seem to appreciate what they have; it is like a refuge or a sanctuary where everyone lives in harmony. `

Rocco felt like talking for a change and just talked about what he had seen within the valley, and the amazing plant life that was unimaginable unless experienced, he continued talking all the way back to the compound where they found some excitement as the Drone had concluded the a semblance of information and was trying to construct legible sentences .

It seems that the warriors or resident creatures had taken offence at some of the pronunciations and were throwing anything they had to hand at the Drone.

Rocco watched with some amusement from some distance and allowed the commotion to continue until the group broke out of the enclosure and started towards him.

He again stood his ground while Ix-Chel started to increase in height. This seemed to cause some panic and the angry mob, recognising that with Ix-Chel, they would have difficulty in getting their own way with the Captain.

Now that they saw how big and aggressive Ix-Chel had become, they stopped dead in their tracks.

Rocco saw panic in their faces as they started to retreat.

His initial thoughts were of compassion; these creatures had had a difficult day and it should be expected that they would be fed up with all the attention.

However, he recognised something else in their demeanour. Yes, it was not the natural way for anyone to act.

They were truly scared and whatever was causing it, was something they feared, far more than Ix-Chel and himself.

This fear had stopped the aggression, brought them to scramble backwards while they trampled over each other trying to get away. Then he caught a glimpse out of the corner of his eye as the tiger emerged from the wooded area and approached Rocco.

He whispered, ` do not move Ix.  Trust me; stand completely still. `

The tiger slowly moved closer toward them and stood next to Rocco's leg as he lowered his hand down to the tigers head and petted it as before.

Then suddenly, it made everyone jump a mile high, as it gave a tremendous blood-curdling roar.

Rocco immediately instructed Ix-Chel to take the local creatures back to their enclosure and help the Drone to sort out its language skills. He then knelt down and embraced his new companion.

` So it wasn't a dream! You really do exist. `

The tiger rubbed its scent pads all over Rocco while he stayed petting the beast for some while; then realising that Tuwa would soon appear, he tried to guide her outwards away from the area. He could not take the risk of his new friend being shot.

Tuwa had been called for because of the emergency breakout and as just as he had suspected, they all arrived fully armed with every weapon they possessed just as the tiger stood up to full height on its rear legs and licked Rocco's face.

Tuwa was horrified and for the first time in his life struck dumb, as Rocco ordered them to back off. Then he turned and walked toward the trees, followed by his furry friend disappearing into the security of the jungle.

It was after some considerable time that Rocco returned, to great sighs of relief from the Ja'Way team. The local residents then surprised everyone by going down on their knees to pay homage to him as a great and powerful leader. He just laughed and smiled as he waved them to get up.

This situation, was getting crazy, it must all stop now. No, Rocco did not want homage or anything like that, he only to go back to his family where everything was calm and reasonably normal.

It was with great relief that things would now become less exciting as the language barrier lifted and the residents made an effort to accommodate their new allies.

The encampment was sparse with some dwellings that amounted to only a few stone blocks, built in a primitive way, but well shaped. The stoneware was forming the base and outer wall of each dwelling and stood approximately one meter high with interwoven tree branches reaching upwards forming a dome with ventilation openings at the apex.

Some of the structures were covered in stretched animal skin, while others (the majority in fact) had layers of palm leafs after all, this was a temperate climate, and perhaps unnecessary to fortify themselves against any harsh weather especially when they had the mountains overlooking and protecting them.

Picket fences had been erected and surrounded the whole community. Rocco thought the fence inadequate, considering the size of his new fury friends but perhaps they had other ways to defend themselves.

He had watched and noticed how the creatures conducted themselves. They appeared inquisitive and to learn quickly about the Mayan crew and in particular Elder.

It reminded Rocco of a story about a colony of people who gave the impression to outsiders, of being lethargic.

They would resist the will of an aggressor showing a passive restraint to any mal-treatment and smile, showing no resentment at all. It was the will of their God.

They appeared to have no defence against anything and passive resistance was not even an option. They would rather die, then jeopardise their beliefs of love, peace, and harmony.

It was found later that these people were mentally stronger than any other known to exist and practised a religious monastic order in a secret and remote place that increased their strength of mind over matter completing a oneness with their ultimate objective of godliness and perfect peace.

It has been said, that they studied their adversaries and destroyed them by using any weaknesses they had against them.

These creatures had not shown any physical signs; but were certainly passive and very secretive with their ways of control and survival. This puzzled Rocco, how could they defend themselves from the animals around them and why the tiger had not been aggressive?

These thoughts led to wondering about other animals that shared the valley and if someone or something had control over them? Then there was the question of the waterfalls, its mystical powers, why was it sacred and why did the local inhabitants all go elsewhere to collect the water? What would happen if it were consumed?   Rocco contacted his friend Tuwa and asked him secretly to collect water samples, so that it could be analyzed on the Invistor Star.

The following day communications started. The Drone's endeavours had at last come to fruition. This was a good sign, ensuring good communications except the locals had discovered that they were being addressed as critters, creatures and other less admirable names.

What followed was the discovery, by the Ja'Way team, that the resident tribe did not actually have a tribal name. So the team leaders decided that it would be appropriate for them to hold a meeting and give them, (if they approved) a proper name.

The gathered members at the meeting found an interesting selection of names and then chose the nearest name from all the main factors of choice; the first being, that they could fly and the second that they had the ability of great speed.

The team's first choice was Lemmings, god knows why. They seemed to find it hilarious and it was seriously nearly accepted except, they could not stop laughing over the joke about the name.

Then someone mentioned the name Sharpei; which Rocco had stated earlier was a name of a long skinned animal that he knew, so Lemming Sharpei was born and the tribe was just about to be christened with that name, using the local water, collected from the waterfall since it was so readily available.

However, the Sharpie resisted, the anointment and it was the first time the crew witnessed a very strong hostility and aggression.

At that time, the team did not know that the water was sacred to the tribe and not drunk because of its special powers. However, the team had a small supply of alcohol and made several long toasts and even managed to squeeze Tuwa into getting some Mayan brandy sent down on the pretext of breaking a bottle, for good luck.

The evening was the first successful collaboration that introduced the Lemming Sharpei to alcohol.

However, it should be noted here and now, that they found this wonderful name a bit of a mouthful and with a majority consensus, they condensed it down to the Sharpei tribe, and the name stuck.

The wonders of pleasant excess, made the night pass quickly, with some happiness and some small arguments between the Sharpei and their own inebriates. Their lack of experience and control of feelings under the influence caused much confusion. Everyone, including the crew took it upon themselves to individually christen all the Sharpie tribe.

 Of course, this could only come about by understanding and although the Drone was given all the compliments, for all its hard work Tuwa and Rocco were grateful that it could not be given alcohol. However, it did give renditions of Rock music as the night progressed, and many renditions of the music on Earth during the years of 1960 were revised at full volume blasting the night away.

As the dawn slowly arrived, nearly everyone had found a place to lay their heads. That is except those that had over indulged who found themselves in a crumbled heap on the roadside with atomic hangovers.

`Perhaps now` Rocco thought, they could relax and enjoy the pleasures that this planet Shambhala had. He had felt that he neglected his family but security was uppermost in his mind. He would not bring anyone down to this village if there were a risk; and Tigers were certainly in that category.

Chapter Thirteen

It was these thoughts in his mind that drew him again to the open space of first meeting.

His excited expectations of meeting the cub and its mother quickened his pace only to be disappointed on arrival.

 The clearing was unusually quiet and empty and his senses teased him in the early morning mist. This was not what he had expected. Why did he feel that he was not alone, like the man mentioned in another story that lived on the street of a thousand eyeballs; or was it something ruder than that?

Rocco edged his way towards a large magnificent tree and stood with his back against it.

Whatever it was out there, he knew that he could not run and hide, but if in real peril he could at least climb.

Today he came armed with laser and knife because he had felt that one singular Tiger was impossible to believe. `After all it takes two to tango and a lot more to sustain a colony. `

He whispered to himself as he wondered what else could resided in the unexplored regions; this valley appeared huge as they passed over head in the shuttlecraft, and now he realised just how big it really was; compared to the area around Victoria falls in Africa this could be three times the size.

A movement in the shadows caught his noticed, something in the long grass and tropical plants. As he watched, the movement became larger as a tiger bounded forward towards him. It was not his friend but a much larger animal and definitely a male; probably the father to the cub that he had befriended and played with.

Suddenly it leapt into the air and landed a few meters away from him stopping sharply.

` Here we go ` he thought, another bloody confrontation, but the tiger seemed to be waiting for something.

Rocco's mind raced at what to do, he did not want to kill it. Perhaps it thought that by leaping into the air, it would make him run and a chase would pursue but Rocco was prepared for that.

Then something happened that he was not prepared for, when two more large males joined the party and all three of them sat in front of him licking their lips exposing their incisors that lay just inside the larger Sabre like canines.

Back at the village, Ix-Chel and Elder had searched in vain for their Captain and the alarm had gone out to the rest of the villagers.

 Captain Lord Tuwa was most concerned. Rocco was his alto ego, they could have been joined at the hip, and like a twin; he could feel the pain, when the other was in distress, but kept all this to himself.

After a complete search of the village and surrounding area, he decided to set a fully armed search party that would scour the valley end to end and God help anyone that got in Tuwa's way.

The party divided into two groups, guided by the new partners the Sharpei. Lord Captain Tuwa then directed that they dissect the valley into two, dividing their forces while he sent runners ahead to speed view the entire valley and report. While the Ja'Way and the Invistor Star, took up positions above the planet scanning each area for life forms.

Rocco's awakening was slow; he believed that he had fallen asleep under the influence of the forest flowers, and expected to see his three friends still watching his every movement while they groomed each other.

Now he found himself in darkness, contained within some sort of box and surprised to feel that it restricted his movements.

Then suddenly he became aware that he was not alone. His eyes had caught the glimpse of a pinhole within the furthest point, well below his feet and it seemed to twinkle. He heard a hiss and suddenly froze. ` Hell what is that? Oh God; don't let it be a snake please.

The twinkle moved again, like an eyelid closing and opening. His fears grew that they had stuck a snake in the box as well.

He struck out with his feet in the hope of crushing it before it could strike, but found nothing.

`Well`, he whispered, ` whatever it is I cannot escape it in here and with the resolution that there was nothing he could do, his mind cleared. Then came the realisation that snakes do not have eyelids. The fear suddenly removed he squeezed his body tight and slowly turned himself on to his chest, drew his knees inwards and upwards beneath him, taking a position where he could lever his back up to the lid of the box and pushed with all his might.

It moved, the top moved with a sharp hiss that now, so determined was he, that he summoned up all his strength, and with a great effort, pushed the lid slowly upwards, sliding it sideways across the outer casing allowing more light and air into the box. With this, he discovers himself to be in a cavern and as he tries to extract himself out of the box, his movement attracts and initiates a flux of power that produces a little low amber light.

Rocco emerges through the opening like a moth metamorphosing, shaking his limbs to induce feeling, then stretching his arms and legs to their fullest; he begins to feel the warm return of his circulation. With his eyes, slowly becoming accustomed to the light he sees many more containers all aligned in a circle around him. Looking down into the box there is nothing except a pinhole in the side and whatever it was that he thought he saw and heard had now gone.

It is now he realises that he has also been encapsulated in a suit that resembles Earths early protection garments, against the elements of space, a pocketed, first layer of a space suit that even now, was still pumping liquid around his extremities as though he were in flight within an area with little, or no atmosphere.

He had seen something similar before at a science museum, but never one that had bodily attachments like this one.

It was with this realization his mind leapt into thinking perhaps it pumped antifreeze or even worse, embalming fluid that made him start to fumble quickly wanting to remove the tubing that he found attached to his body. Then a small noise attracted his attention, as a slither of tin plating rattled down to the floor, followed by an Android, who appeared from a damaged shell of a craft that had certainly seen better days.

The Android was not one of his, but a battered semblance of bits and pieces crudely put together. He felt sorry for it as it struggled to approach him and began to realise   that it was speaking to him in machine language. ` It was alarmed that he did not know about removing the healing fluids. He must not remove the tubes; any diversion from the correct procedure would mix the two separate prescriptions and the result would kill him! `

He understood, of course the principles would not be anything like, what they had back on Earth and as it continued chattering on, it was clear that it had mistaken him for its missing Captain that, the remaining crew had been searching for. His disappearance following the crash had alarmed the whole crew; they seemed unable to manage without a leader. Then some later time, it had picked up

Rocco's vital life signs while he was engaged with some of the local animals, and the Android had assumed that he had been attacked.

The Android seemed totally unaware of time, or how long it had been waiting for the Captain to be found, since many of its components were missing. However, it knew events had taken place realising it was the last member of the team still active. It assumed command, obeyed the main directive to assist when life is in danger, imbedded deep within its memory banks.

Rocco learns that the Android had transported him from the meeting place of the tigers, into their sanctuary within the heart of a mountain. `This was the maximum distance that the crumbling transporter could manage in its present state. `

This Android was almost human in its attitude towards him; it had missed the company and daily order of the domestic life within the spacecraft, it seemed genuinely pleased to not be alone anymore. ` So, even machines have needs, ` he thought.

The Cavern lighting slowly brightened, its amber glow struggled into becoming a lighter orange shade that trembled from lack of use. `Whatever power they were using to generate the light must be from some sort of atomic power. ` He thought. ` They had determined that their position and condition, was as most star ships in peril, kept at alert readiness for any situation in any strange environment.

However, it seems after some time, the crew had decided to return to their box type capsules, to conserve energy perhaps. Then, when the energy had failed or become unsafe, the exposure penetrated everything except the mechanicals in this small, tight, cavern and they had all died probably from radiation poisoning.

Rocco looked to identify the contents of all the boxes or capsules and found that they contained the resemblance of life forms and realised that whatever had been keeping them alive, had long since departed or closed down.

He was surprised to find that, there appeared to be only skeletal remains and remarkably, they were wearing similar flight suits that he found himself dressed in.

Each skeleton was adorned with unusual items of personal jewellery and he presumed that they had, during their short lives, gathered great wealth and were obviously protecting their interests by wearing it.

His real worry now was why they were already so badly decomposed that only the bones remained.

Rocco was beginning to realise   that he too was in danger from over exposure and began furtively searching for a way out. He searched each passage and every cavern looking for some clue or opening followed by the clanking and chattering android.

Chapter Fourteen

 He eventually came to an area of stored provisions and another outlet that led to a series of small chambers, where he found another box-capsule hidden away. It contained the body of a child and amazingly, still alive in deep sleep mode within the hibernation capsule.

The young child was facially drawn showing a slender skeleton of crinkled skin in obvious stages of hypothermia. It was not certain whether it was a boy or girl but he could see it was urgent to get a team down to either remove the child or arrange for the whole pod to go as one and deliver it in a triangular collection to the Ja'way then straight over to the Invistor Star's medical installation.

Rocco asked the Android to start arranging for the child to be disconnected, so that the capsule was ready to be transported. He explained that it was a matter of great urgency and that they must all leave this place immediately. He went on to ask about how and where the main fuselage of the ship was, hoping that the forced entry it had made, had not collapsed the mountains vertical exit.

The Captain and the Android made a comical sight standing side by side examining the main fuselage but by luck or chance Rocco's life signs had been picked up by the Star and a familiar voice whispered in his ear, ` are you all right darling. `

The angelic tones of her voice stunned him for just a second, (she felt his pause) he could feel his eyes watering and his respiration quicken. It may have been the contamination effecting him that, contributed to his melancholia. His feelings that caused him to cry or the fact that he, Appi and little April had been separated far longer than ever before and despite this new adventure he only wanted to get back to them and his beloved Star.

` Hello my love, ` his voice had a gentle tremble as he whispered and transferred his thoughts with a mental picture to Appi; it was quicker than trying to explain it verbally.

The situation, she understood immediately was critical, she closed her eyes as his thoughts reached her and focused on his finding the child and its metal companion.

When able to speak, he explained. ` Appi, We must leave here as quickly as possible, we are contaminated from radiation poisoning. ` Suddenly just as he finished, a large black shadow covered the mountainous area exactly above where they hoped to escape, and the life support coffin holding the child, gentle lifted upwards as a tractor beam pulled it out to safety, leaving two transporter rings in its place. By the time, Rocco had snapped one onto the Drone and the other on his own finger they were back on the Ja'way and immediately transferred again directly to sick quarters on the Invistor Star.

The child and Rocco succumbed to nurse Chat-a-Lot's charms, who prepared them both for immersion. But Rocco, laughingly escaped, because he was found to be just on the edge of the red borderline, the safe limit for total exposure.

The child now removed from its box was dying and required the full treatment of the fabulous pink jelly, to restore life giving replacement acids and healing properties.

However, this treatment required the full immersion into a large glass tube and a mask small enough for the child to breathe with was unavailable until the chief Android conjured up a homemade one.

This futuristic system totally unknown on Earth would be so beneficial to everyone, so long as one did not suffer from claustrophobia. In this case, however, the child would have no idea that it had been subjected to suspended animation within the test tube as Rocco liked to call it.

Everyone hoped that it would make a fast recovery, despite the damages to some vital organs. The jelly held special properties and if they were in time, it would eventually progress in the removal of all the impurities accumulated internally and externally, from the exposure in the cavern.

As the days passed on the star, the visits from his old friends became less frequent.

Lord Tuwa and Tepintri had taken a more active interest in the new planet of Shambhala that his new mother in law had christened. Elder and Ix-Chel were engaged in the discoveries of new customs connected with the Sharpei tribe who were being given encouragement to learn the Mayan language and shown how to protect themselves.

Rocco meanwhile, was enjoying the comforts and pleasures of fatherhood, with his beloved Appi and April. He had returned to his old self except that he missed the company of Tepintri and Ix-Chel even though they had become more difficult to hide within his secret thoughts.

If ever a man dreamed of perfect sexual bliss these two women `he thought` could actually kill him with extreme unlimited satisfaction. Secretly he loved them both but, a different type of love; perhaps it was just lust, wishful thinking, because he adored his one true love Appi and even more his beautiful daughter. She brought out his true adoration as she glowed with a rainbow aura of goodness and beauty crawling towards him:

` You know Appi my love, if I have any more happiness my whole being will explode. ` Appi laughed as she scooped up the little one. ` I also feel just as you` she exclaimed, ` it sometimes feels too much to endure my husband. I pray we will not die from this excess of happiness. ` Both laughed and burst out even more when the door to their quarters opened and standing before them was nurse Chat-a-lot in all her glory. ` Come on, come on my dears. ` Chat-a-lot had now acquired a Cornish accent that made them burst out loud again with laughter and tears. ` My dears, ` she went on, ` you ave a visitor waiting, ` she continued, ` please be a moving you down, to the lounge my deario's. `

Appi, reluctantly passed the bemused April to Chat-a-lot and tried to scold Rocco for altering the nurse's voice patterns.

Both Captains made their way to the reception lounge to find the chief android from the science laboratory waiting patiently.

` My Captains I have news of the infant, I would like you both to attend the meeting of assessment and advise us on the best way to proceed. `

Rocco noted that the Android was in a very solemn state of mind, unusually so, and Appi picked up her husband's thoughts; guessing that the child had grave problems and perhaps all their efforts of trying to save the child would now come to nothing.

The doors parted as they approached the isolation ward and at first glance, it appeared that all was well. The Android started gathering up the notes of the experiments they had undertaken to assist the child's recovery. He stopped and looking straight at the two Captains. `This child my Captains; is not fully identifiable, nor could it be registered into male or female category, it is very unusual because, it displays both genitalia.

Appi and Rocc looked strangely at each other then looked at the child. Appi spoke first ` How could such a beautiful little baby be both male and female? I have never heard of such a thing. ` Rocco smiled ` Oh, but I have my love, I don't think it is such a common thing but, hermaphrodite, I have heard of. You know there are some species that can reproduce without a partner. ` Appi becomes very quiet and looks back at the child.

` But, it seems so completely normal and natural. So peaceful in this suspended state and you say that it is definitely showing signs of improvement. `

The Android continued ` Yes, and it is curious, as you say, it looks like any other child except the sex and the two-notched lumps on its back. ` The medical team are unsure whether they were an abnormality for this particular race of people.

They believe that there is no discomfort. However, the purpose for these lumps is unknown; but he assured them it would eventually come to light and be understood later, perhaps in the future. For the present they would remain a mystery perhaps for some time and then, only time would tell.

There was a long pause; `We have made some repairs to the attendant Drone and from what they had gathered from further interrogation the tribal name could be Airieons, from a planet that is not classified on our star charts .

We understand that after losing their Captain outside the crash site, they had taken to drinking the sacred water that flowed through the mountain passages.

Rocco's face turned grey. This area of drinking the sacred water was already known to be a crime punishable by the highest possible penalty. Nevertheless, perhaps under these extreme circumstances, they could argue the death penalty point with the Sharpei elders.

`My Captains, What we have now discovered is perhaps the most difficult problem. Our Invistor science team, have established that the water contains a new life form, a Gold Nano species of intelligent Microsones which join metallically together in a process that enables fast productivity. It is possible that the Airieon crew unwittingly fed the child the water to sustain it. Alternatively, there is a strong possibility that the Nanos may have gathered within either the mother or child during the child's containment of pregnancy.

In either case, it was found that these Nanos replace bone structures and since they are constructed in Gold, they would never degrade. ` The chief Android paused,

`That is to say, whilst we are familiar with carbon based animals having a calcium built bone structure, these Nano's will naturally replace the bones in time, leaving a golden metallic skeleton with indestructible joints, that continue to grow by regenerative reconstruction.

 `We have found that the microscopic Nanos, replace themselves with new as the structure grows, just like bones but in this case, aged Nanos are digested by the new and regenerated.

All other muscles and sinews remain as in the human or any Carbon based form except, with a difference of blood. That has been replaced by a cocktail concoction of oily liquids, produced by the Airieon's unusual digestive system. Our preliminary investigations have shown that foremost, amongst other things, the circulating liquid; contains the oils from cetacean blubber and fats from several oceanic species of fish and Seal that are blended with an unknown type of vegetable oil. This combination of liquids would allow the Airieon species to survive great temperature changes below the point of freezing.

This is a life form that may only die if deconstructed and separated from its parts by some distance, since the Nano's will continue to divide and form more just like a virus. They will continue to build even after the receptive body is dead, or until the circulating oil mixture evaporates, leaks or runs out, causing a seizure of its metallic parts by overheating. `

Rocco and Appi were shocked at this disclosure and now wondered whether it was safe to have this creature around.

`Now; I begin to understand, ` started Rocco, ` why the water is so special and why that the Sharpei would not allow us access to test it. Their ancestors and I mean those elected as leaders or priests, must have used the powers of the water to extend their life, hoping to be around forever. We must make a decision, as fast as possible about whether to let the alien child live; or dispense with it now, while it is still under sedation. `

This would require an emergency meeting; both Captains agree that all the main principles of both planets should assemble in the guest lounge as soon as possible. Rocco ordered the Android to arrange all ships officers, including Ix-Chel and Elder to represent the shadows. Rocco thought it not expedient to exclude the Sharpei leaders because of the water law.

The emergency gathering caused some excitement amongst the assembled members and as refreshments were not forthcoming, everyone started to take their places around a large table in the centre of the room.

` Captain Rocco appears to have gone into a trance, ` Tepintri whispers into Appi's ear. `

He continues to stare blankly into the distance until suddenly reawakening as Appi nudges his side with her elbow.

` Appi, I think ` Rocco begins to air his thoughts ` things are coming together at last; ` I believe the tigers are being manipulated by the Nano's; after all, they would originally have no idea about the contents of the water, and must have used it to drink at some time or other. If they were contaminated; It would explain their size, their interest in us and their passive actions. They are it seems, intelligent and the child is probably in a similar condition. It too would be just as intelligent, and defiantly at one with all life, that has

taken the water. My God, this explains so many things. `
`Except`, said Lord Tuwa seated at the head of the table who stammers and repeats; `Except, we still don't know, who planted the mystery vines!!

He continues; `Now to the point, if we colonise this area, the water supply that is used by our friends the sharpie, will not be enough for you all. Then we must consider the valley's vegetation perhaps it too is contaminated. I refer to the unusual plant life and the strange but wonderful displays at night that release drug inducing florescence for the Micro life that pollinates the flowers. `

At this point , Rocco raises his hands and starts to address the meeting. `On the other hand, we could if they agreed and allowed us to settle, join the Sharpei. With all our advanced techniques, experience and modern tools, I am sure an arrangement could easily be made to filter and retain a separate water depository, just for us. `

Tuwa jumped to his feet, `I cannot in all honesty understand why my home on Mayan is not acceptable? We are not only friends but also family and we have a committed alliance. There is so much to achieve on Mayan and what about the treasures in the City of Atlantis with so much, still to learn and be discovered beneath the sea. `

The room suddenly bussed with excited chatter. Tuwa tried again `Gentlemen,- Ladies. ` He starts to raise his voice ` We have worked miracles together and now we have control of all three planets. What a force we can be, if we all come together, Moofee, Shadows, Sharpei, Mayans, and Freedom all under one command. We can accomplish so much as a team and control the area with our fleet. `

It was here that Appi interjected. ` Please we must not forget that my people are waiting on the home planet of Moofee; they are risking everything on us to help them escape from the imminent danger of a Super Nova. We have enough transport here to collect thousands, the urgency is to decide where to settle a whole nation, not just those of us gathered here!!

 I think the risks of infection by Nano's are far less important than the complete destruction of our planet. `   Quietness descended on the meeting.

 Rocco deliberated that they should stay together as a nation it would not be right to divide the community between three planets, After all the Moofee nation could easily take any planet by force if they wanted to, but they chose not.

He went on, ` let us be sensible, the newly named planet of Shambhala, needs people to live on it and work on it. It needs all the care and attention of a sophisticated nation that would inspire trade and friendship. The resident animals need a community they can trust and we have already shown that. The indigenous people; our friends the Sharpei get on very well with all of us.

` Rocco makes a pause and smiles at Ix-Chel and Elder. ` Now please let's get back to the main reason for this meeting; what shall we do with the child?

The assembly of dignitaries and leaders suddenly found the lounge they were gathered in, becoming darker as a great shadow passed across the Star ship. They waited patiently for the annoyance to disappear, but the room slowly became darker. Then suddenly everything went completely black.

A nervous laugh broke the tense atmosphere, as a voice cried out it is an omen of doom the prophecy. Alarms started to ring in the accustomed way, ending in a crescendo of smashed glass. The meeting broke up in disarray. A voice in the darkness could be heard shouting, ` put the lights on someone, 'but, in the excitement there was a mad rush for a door. Then, someone fell and others followed, causing a mass of strewn bodies, blocking the exit, and access to the lighting control boxes that used infrared sensors.

It was standard practise, perhaps for the purposes of economy that the lighting only came on after the detection of someone entering the area, but because this area was seldom used someone had turned the mains switch off.

Chapter Fifteen

Captains Rocco and Appi, still seated at their conference table, received a mental message from the chief Android in the Star's control centre. Who announced, that, ` A disturbance in the area had twitched one of the largest moons surrounding the white dwarf to alter its position? He gripped his teeth as a new message relayed from Control informed him that this in turn had nudged a unnamed smaller moon, causing instability and pushing it forward into a position that now caused an eclipse.
`Captain, ` The Android went on; this moving objects position is altering as I speak and is now on a degrading spiral being drawn directly into the sun, Appi realizing the complexity of the situation turned to Rocco; `For God's sake Rocc, just as we thought that all my people could leave Moofee this happens. How does a planet, that has been stable, for god knows how many years, suddenly decide to move? This is not a good sign; it looks as though Tuwa will get his wish, we may all have to leave and restart from the beginning all living together as one big family on Mayan. `
The lights returned and found everyone except Rocco on the floor for safety. Rocco began to explain the situation to Tuwa and what the Androids had predicted. Sawston was the first to ask whether anything could be done and how long they thought they had.
 Rocco smiled, you know, it looks like a planet, moves like a planet therefore we assume it must be a planet; but, why and how is it sitting in one place. This thing defies all the laws of gravitational pull and movement. If it is a planet, I cannot believe there is a star ship known that can obliterate an entire planet. How do you remove a planet? ` He inquired. ` If we

blasted it, that would only destroy a small area and could be pulled into the Sun causing even more problems. `

Rocco knew that they had to try something because if the whole planet actually degraded and touched the Sun, the result would be to destroy the whole of this Galaxy.

I suppose it is possible to make the Sun move it, but let's discuss this. To Nuke the Sun, in a particular area, would in turn certainly produce, giant multiple Solar flares and perhaps more radiation than we can handle. However, the flares in turn, may push it away but, who can say how far? `

The arguments came nervously fast with people becoming more and more frantic. There were more questions than answers. In fact, the atmosphere in the room was so bad, that some, decided not to wait and find out, by departing the Invistor Star, to escape what they thought to be the end of everything.

A new message of confirmation came down from control.

Rocco moaned, `Oh God please let it be good news. `

Perhaps God had heard him. Reluctantly he asked the Android to relay the information over the speaker system. Why he should be the bearer of all the bad news, he thought to himself.

`Captain ` the Android at the control centre started; `The planet has now completely stopped, all movement has ceased. ` They ran to look at the impossible. It just hung there, totally eclipsing the sun revealing only its dark side towards them.

As they watched, a glitter of light revealed itself from within a great chasm that exploded initially, just like a volcano, sending its lava running into a canyon. Then the planet appeared to burst, revealing extreme light across the full horizontal width of the outer surface, producing what appeared to be an implosion of light.

At first, everyone thought that the centre of the planet had melted inwardly away, allowing the Sun to break through and disperse the eclipse through the centre.

Rocco commented, `it looks like a giant doughnut oozing cream out of the centre. ` But his words were lost in the cries of the frightened people. Slowly the light settled into a regular shape, ending around the perimeter edges of that facing side of the planet.

It became a picture frame shape, as if holding a white unprepared canvas tightly stretched across and above the facia. It slowly produced guidelines and shapes on the canvas that began to colour, ending in a portrait of a giant face appearing in full Technicolor, filling the entire extremities of the planets one side.

`Its God! Its God ` The cry went up. Panic now became terror, as people dropped to their knees, re-claiming their beliefs for this their judgement day.

Appi was under the table pulling on Rocco's jacket for him to join her. (As if that would protect him) But, Rocco took an objectionable stance. ` This can't be God ` he declared; ` Why would God send a globe with a face on it? Why would he need a planet anyway? `

Rocco sat bolt upright, holding his ridged position, staring in defiance ` Listen, God is all powerful. ` He declared. ` He doesn't need to travel around on a globe showing his face. `

Leaping to his feet Rocco shouted; ` Red alert - Battle stations. ` He thumped the table with his fist and transferred his thoughts to the Command section. ` Prepare all missiles and fire on my command. `

Rocco and Appi now running to the communication section, gave orders to send a message out to God in all known languages; ` This is the Battle Star ship Invistor. You have two minutes to move your position, away from the Sun and surrender; or be destroyed.

The planet face did not respond, and the time lapse made the crew feel as though time had actually stopped. They silently watched and waited and the more they looked at the face the more menacing it seemed.

Rocco watched the minute hand hit five minutes on his watch, and again ordered the messages to be re-sent and to continue

being sent. But nothing happened.

That's it, he declared the waiting is over as he commanded the Invistor Star to move away from its position to one side, giving access and full view between the eclipsing planet and the Sun.

Then, he gave the command. `FIRE, ` everyone watched and gasped as the six large nuclear missiles sped directly to the Sun's nearest trajectory to the offending planet.

The explosion was massive and blindingly more than he expected, as the sun produced a tsunami of a solar flux, a storm of death that hit the offending planet so hard, that it moved it backwards as it engulfed it with fire.

The Invistor Star now faced a backlash from the build up of atomic force. The momentum of the blast started to move the ship backwards to a position well away from the area of massive destruction. The team watched the radioactive measurements twitching upwards while displayed on their computer screens. The figures   reached and passed the critical points as everyone held their breaths, until slowly the fallout began to dissipate, as it was sucked away by the vacuum of space and time into the mysterious black matter.

Appi, ordered the protective command screens to be closed, as the main force of the blast drew closer, and noted as she watched through the closing slit, that the giant face had began to melt. She whispered `So God is not infallible; ` NO. ` Replies, Rocco. ` He's not inflammable either. `

The quests started to appear in the corridor outside the control room. Some had not quite recovered from their devotional shock and continued with their religious pleading, while others gave multiple prayers of forgiveness. But, there were those that had been against the action he had taken, they were murmuring amongst themselves about the consequences of the Captains drastic actions. It was obvious, their thoughts turned to retribution, and how they were going to defend themselves against the wrath of God.

 The crowd, increasing in numbers, gathered tightly at the entrance, showing great hostility and as Rocco turned to console them, he heard the words. `Murderer, Murderer; you have killed God. `
It started as a quiet cry and taken up as a chant, as some of the crew from the Ja'Way joined the visitors.
The situation looked threatening and they seemed ready to personally attack Rocco and his family. However, the Drones picked up his feelings of anxiety, and had already acted upon directions from the chief Android, who, with foresight had pre- assembled all the Drones into a defensive position at the front and rear of the baying crowd. It was then; after some gentle prodding, with a few mild electrical shocks, stimulating the weak minded, that the over excited crowd, slowly begin to quieten and came to understand that the Captain, was still in charge and still holding the upper hand.
Rocco calmly made a statement about what he had done and why he believed, it necessary to take the action that he had. He Emphasized, ` GOD, does not need a planet with his face leering out at  passing spacecraft. `The silent crowd permitted him to continue. ` Listen everyone. God is all-powerful; he created everything. Isn't that what we have all been taught to believe? ` He paused again.

` My friends, this was a false diversion by someone or something with a plan. It made the face and probably made this satellite too. It resembles a planet and from what I have seen of it, was constructed very well. But, it was not made as other planets and appears to be hollow for some reason. We may never know why, until we have investigated the remaining debris.

It may have been around here for many, many years tucked up within the other moons. Watching and learning about this whole area including the inhabitants of all the planets. ` He continued ` In any case it was certainly dangerous and if it had connected with the Sun, none of us would be alive now.

The consequences would be total annihilation. So, for the present we have avoided that.

We will study what is left of the debris after the Radioactivity and contamination have dispersed. Let's give the Sun time to calm down. ` He nodded to the chief Android. ` Please take these people to the reception lounge and keep them there until it's safe to transfer them back to their own planets. `

Rocco turned and resumed his duties at the Command centre; the Drones were taking account of the damages to the ship. While examining the external cameras they found that some of them were still actively working. They had survived the blast, giving the team an opportunity to study the floating debris. Some of the remains were still intact with large bulky pieces floating in a rotational whirl around the waiting Sun or perhaps for some solar wind to disperse them.

The unnamed planet was remarkable in the sense that it was not a natural planet or moon but totally made by the hand of something or some person for a reason not yet discovered.

The power of the Sun's wrath, enflamed with the missiles had smashed the sphere. It may have, in its original state fuelled   the sun into exploding and releasing an even greater power that would have certainly destroyed the assembled fleet surrounding it.

As for the planets of Mayan and Freedom, the destruction to their surface would have been devastating.

Now however, it had unexpectedly left some interesting items that were protected by strong unknown elements or alloys that would hold signatures or evidence from other planets and perhaps scientific items of great interest.

Rocco had the larger remains pulled in with the tractor beam that after decontamination, were found to contain remnants of specimens from the planet Shambhula.

The team found that in amongst the secured archives, collected after the devastation of the Sphere were copies of a stone tablet that had not been seen by the Captains of the Invistor Star or other members and friends from the Moofee Nation's expedition. This item was removed and taken away for translation by the chief Android, because it appeared to sanctify the truth of the words written on a plaque that was currently displayed as a historical document, secretly written by the Mayans for their historical archive.

It was sometime before the chief Android returned with the documents and declared.   ` Captains, this is a synopsis of what is written. It records and documents events of our arrival at this galaxy and covers over forty pages of frequent and repetitive statements. I have transcribed this for your perusal.

Chapter Sixteen

The great charter: describing the conflict between the Planet of Mayan, and the Moofee Barbarians.

Here it is written:
 During the Great War of Mayan; that started on the 2nd day, of the Metorni month, in the year 8000, of the Tunati Tecknoc calendar.
 A historic battle took place within the air space of the planet of Mayan, where the Lord Defender Tuwa Tonati-uh, resisted an attack of great strength, and defeated the Great Lord Captain Rocco of Moofee.
It is recorded here, how the great Lord Tunati, descendant of Tunarti-uh the Magnificent; delivered the Mayan people from tyranny and slavery.
The Captain of the great Battleship, The Invistor Star, overwhelmed with superior forces sent out a messenger in a small shuttlecraft to make parley with the invincible Mayan leader, Lord Tuwa Tonati-uh.
The great Lord Tuwa Tonati-uh, gave no respite to the Aliens, who`s strength melted from the arguments of force that followed.
After hours of lengthy deliberations and demands, that concluded with the messenger handing over his shuttlecraft and surrendering the mighty Battleship, The Invistor Star, with all its crew to the army of Mayan.
The Lord Tuwa Tunati-uh, sealed the accord, by forcing the messenger to climb out, of his craft, carrying a white flag, the symbol of their surrender.
This action; was witnessed by the assembled Army on the planet of Mayan. Where great jubilation took place as the

messenger was urged to march up and down on the roof of the spacecraft.

Our illustrious Leader, Lord Tuwa Tonati-uh, then returned to his personal shuttlecraft and without fear entered: The great Battleship Invistor Star, where he presented the terms of surrender to their Lord Commander Rocco of Moofee.

Appi glanced at Rocco who just smiled. ` I hope he has got lots of that Mayan brandy because it will take some many evenings to explain this one. `

Rocco retired to his private den, he did not want to be disturbed. All these strange adventures and happenings over the last week or so had revolved into a circle that seemed to gather momentum and speed on ever faster, with no sign of ever stopping. Everyday had new problems to solve, the valley with the Sharpei, the tigers, crashed space ships, and now the mystery sphere had come into their lives.

He deduced in these quiet moments that only a specialist with structural engineering experience would be able to estimate the magnetic requirements against the structural weight, for such a sphere to remain in orbit, without it crashing down to the planet's surface. He listened to his own thoughts, as he voiced aloud; `This feat of engineering was certainly a wondrous achievement. Made by a civilisation of great technical knowledge, who ` (now walking and talking, taking great strides around the room) ` would certainly return, if only to collect their sphere then move it to another place. ` His thoughts moved on, ` They could use the knowledge already gathered, to attempt to gain control of the surrounding planets grabbing everything. I would! ` He stated. His voice reverberated around the metallic walls of the den. He enjoyed the sound; it boosted his senses still deep in thought, while he untangled his mind. Rocco drifted back to thinking about the Tigers, and wondered what they were doing, he could smell their aroma and sensed suddenly a whiff of a reminder of the flora, with its intoxicating perfume that snapped his thoughts, breaking his concentration, and realising he was not alone.

Then, he heard and recognised the guttural, purring sound, now so familiar and comforting. `Tomorrow Ix, we shall check the state of decontamination with the larger debris that we have collected. If it is safe, we shall discover what secrets they have, hidden on the broken planet.

I think it would be a good idea for Tuwa to make a quick trip to the mountain crash site. I am afraid that you must not go because of the contamination levels a so high. ` She growls. `

Yes, I know but they have special clothing and they can stay for a short time without risk. She nuzzled up to him and purred with the pleasure of his touch as they both stretched out on the visitors couch. It was how they started and how they always relaxed in each other's company in peace and harmony.

Early the following day a small gathering of Drones marched single file into the shuttle bay area where the space debris was contained. A few of the Drones started to break up the larger pieces, while others were sifting and collecting anything that would show who or what had been using the sphere. It was not long before they discovered the remains of a small laboratory where animal experiments had taken place.

Then under some plastic sheeting, they found some horrific remains of a tiger. It had been dissected and all that was left was its head and some neck.

Initially it was thought that it had been killed and used for food but on close examination, it showed signs of Nano infection around the skull where, a golden coating of interlocked Nanos had layered themselves around the cranium, strengthening and protecting the brain. As a Drone completely removed the rest of the covering it exposed more of the remaining neck and shoulder That made Rocco go cold.

Attached onto the lower neck was an artificial pump with a supply valve, which amazingly was transferring a flow of liquid from a recycling container to the brain.

Rocco was horrified. Could this, be the missing mother that they had searched for? He suddenly felt sick and very angry as he started to cover the head; when he saw the eye move. ` My god it is still alive he exclaimed. ` But then he thought he heard something whisper within his head. ` Kill me, please I beg you. Please, Kill me. `

Rocco turned to see if anyone else heard the voice, but he was alone and again the words came to him ` Kill me. `

Rocco drew his knife and disconnected the liquid supply, then plunged the knife into the animal's brain.

The head shuddered and its eyes looked straight at him. Now he was sure, it was his friend and his thoughts were confirmed as it licked his hand and closed its eyes. But, it did not die! ` What inhuman bastard has done this? ` He spoke out loud as he plunged the knife again and again, deep into the head, realising that the animal would not receive peace until it was destroyed. He must use his gun, to disintegrate all the Nano particles and scatter them outside the ship, to be drawn by the pull of the Sun.

With this thought, he attached himself to a safe line for external working and ordered all the Drones out of the Service bay. Then, taking the head to the centre area between the inner and outer exit doors, he pulled himself back, and then closed the inner door. He was now isolated enough to place the head into the best position at the opening point.

He ordered the bay door to be opened on his command and drew his gun, setting it to the maximum kill position. Rocco waited for the all clear to be sounded, then gave the command, and watched the door opened slowly. He waited until just before there was enough room for the head to pass through and fired.

The command to close the door was given immediately; he could not risk the danger of everything including himself, being pulled out. But Luckily, Rocco had remembered the rope as the suction pulled him forward. However, he noted with satisfaction that the tigers head had completely disintegrated and watched it being sucked out into the blackness of the vacuum.

He stood, for a second; shocked, gasping for air, with tears in his eyes. This was a dreadful thing, they had done. The cub would have no mother to guide it and he had lost an amazing friend. He felt as if it were a member of his own extended family and vowed that he would search for the cub and take it to safety.

Sometime later, when normality resumed they found another compartment, which had within it a sealed containment area. It had a strange device that looked exactly like a headset. It was positioned, over a fixed table, with restraining straps.

 Rocco did not like this at all, it reminded him of his first days encounter on the Invistor Star when a security Drone electrocuted him. ` Could this, be a similar device, used for recovery; or more likely used for brainwashing?

He remembered, the painful days of suffering that he went through, it was touch and go for him. Could these people, also be developing the minds of animals or is it just simply, extracting information by torture?

The thoughts of his tiger friend and its suffering brought on a heartfelt depression and continued to bother his conscience. In his mind's eye, he thought constantly about the plea for help. Was it a possible communication? Did he imagine it? These thoughts brought an extraordinary passionate feeling of guilt and hatred towards these sphere living bastards.

Of course, Rocco was no angel; he had killed many times before but, finding his furry friend still alive, after such punishment without its body, outraged him.

He knew that it had suffered and would have continued to suffer for god knows how long, without any chance of finality.

It was later in another larger chunk of the sphere; they found a computer storage bank that must hold millions of computer records that may reveal their science projects. In another part of the recovered fragments, they also discovered a secret partition, again concealed behind a platinum device that defied recognition or purpose.

It resembled a flexible glittering seaweed shape that appeared to be trying to capture his head as it hung precariously from the ceiling. He supposed the possibility of other attachments may be required to ensure it exists in a foreign environment or it might have a need for a different specific power for whatever it is or does.

However, he thought, ` If these aliens have it; it can't be good.

The investigation lasted for nearly a week each piece disassembled, checked, and discarded.

Tuwa at this time had taken a team down to Shambhala, several times using his transporter. They entered all the caves, investigating the crashed vehicle and all the storage items looking for clues.

The spacecraft was found to have a recording device that was still connected to a computer.

Since the visit had only limited time to avoid exposure. The team established a link between the craft and the Ja'Way then transferred all the stored information.

Tuwa was delighted to find in one section of a cave, a number of Drone parts, neatly stacked aside ready for transportation. He hoped they could be reassembled to make another Drone. It was his greatest desire to get one for his own ship.

On their return to the Ja'Way, Tuwa and Sawston realised that the flight recorder found at the rear of the craft, needed specialist adaption to their equipment and a Galaxy class translator. So that was also removed and taken. All the other parts were mostly personal items, with some Star charts. These charts had an as semblance of Script written in a strange way similar to hieroglyphics and a mixture of Mayan.

The situation on the Invistor Star had calmed down considerably, as they travelled back to meet the Ja'Way. It had been agreed that they would travel together back to Mayan, where the other ship The Aparsuent was moored with Captain Smiley.

Lord Tuwa had arranged a family gathering at his home. He had already contacted Rocco to make sure that he would be able to examine what they had found and asked to bring a Drone for translations and help them understand these charts of another world in another Galaxy.

 Captain Appi seemed quite excited; she expressed the hope, that some of the mysteries would be solved once they had put all the evidence together. She loved a mystery.

'It's strange, ` she remarked, `that the sphere was empty as far as they could tell, I wonder what happened to the previous residents? Had they been discovered and removed? Perhaps they had settled on the new planet of Shambhala. Hey, she jibed perhaps they, had planted the vines ? `

Returning to the medical section to get news of the child; they made light talk as they walked along hand in hand like teenage lovers. Rocco laughed. ` Anything is possible my love, ` However, one thing I know for sure, is that someone or thing released the sphere and unless there are other signs of life on the remaining planet or its surrounding moons then, it is plausible my dear Watson? `

Appi thought for a while; `I know most of names around here my husband, but; who is Watson? ` Her eyes half closed she stared quizzingly at him. `Do you have yet another friend that's invisible to me? ` They arrived giggling at nurse Chat-a-lot's domain. She had already anticipated their arrival and stood with the door open; `Welcome my Captains, I have some news. ` She ushered them in to a bright reception room that led on to the main sickroom. ` The child has made some improvement and you may visit. ` Nurse guided them into the special ward; Rocco knew it well, since he was the previous resident.

The room was in semi darkness but they could see the child easily as it lay uncovered from the waist up. Its torso, was strangely illuminated with the floral colours displayed on the plants in the forest.

As they approached, the lighting increased and they both gasped. ` Appi whispered `Rocc it has grown. It's twice the size and is beginning to fill out. ` The child did not speak, but its eyes followed them as they approached the bed.

`Nurse,` Rocco asked, ` has the patient spoken yet? `

` NO,` my Captain dear. ` He turned and spoke directly to Appi ` Perhaps we should get the new Drone to try and talk to the child. If, they have finished repairing it, of course!! ` Appi nodded.

Leaving the surgery, both Captains decided it was time to join the party down on the planet. All the family would be there and Rocco reflecting as he joked, that with any luck Lord Tuwa would have stopped talking by the time they arrived.

` You know my love this is possibly the only time that I have no regrets about the transporter. I mean being without one of course.  By the time we get there, Tuwa will have run out of huff and puff. `

` Appi agreed as she corkscrewed into another seat. The shuttle unsteadily wobbled, alarming the Drone navigator that squealed at high volume as it reached the landing area. Then it bounced its way to a stop.

` Who's driving this thing? ` Rocco shouted. Appi thought it may be one of the Drones that he had given lessons to; until, Tepintri alighted from the pilot's cabin.

`Oh my god, ` Appi was shaken and surprised that Tuwa's wife had learnt to fly a shuttle. Rocco laughed so hard he had to be helped off the ship as the beautiful Tepintri reverted to Ix-Chel the Mayan.

He had wondered why she kept disappearing; now he knew and was impressed that she had shown such determination to become one of them.

` She will make a wonderful pilot, ` he stuttered and chuckled to himself as both ladies took an arm each and escorted him to the party.

Lord Tuwa had been busy, arranging and assembling some long tables, that displayed items deemed as safe from contamination, everything that they had brought back was on view, just like a come and buy sale. Several weapons, that may or may not work if anyone could establish how to use them, all sorts of strange tools and several body suits that Rocco had the misfortune to be fitted with previously. Other mechanical devices that looked like advance engineering, were neatly arranged, but meant very little to Tuwa. His priority was the Drone spares.

Rocco stood stroking his chin, ` I see  `. said Rocco, `
you've got quite a collection, I'll get one of our people to try and assemble what you have . We might be lucky and manage a whole one. `

It was strange that Rocco always referred to the Drones as people. He had supposed that with all the human attributes, he had installed in them that they were now just like him.
Rocco watched Tuwa's face light up with expectation. Then he spotted the charts and quickly unrolled the first one.
` These symbols are very strange; does anyone recognise anything from around this Galaxy? `
He did not really expect an answer since he had only thought about Appi and himself as travellers until Captain Smiley interrupted. `Rocco, ` Smiley started to turn one of the charts around ` this perimeter looks familiar, I can't be certain but it looks like it could be on the very edge of a Galaxy that borders the great blackness of our furthest exploration. I need to overlay it with ours. Can I do this tomorrow? ` He looked directly at Tuwa for approval, in case he now claimed finder's rights to ownership of the charts.

Tuwa nodded and Rocco smiled as he informed them that the Drone, he had brought back from the mountain, could be fully functional again sometime the next day. ` He can explain the charts and our child progeny. Which I must point out is alive and growing at tremendous speed. We must all make a decision as to its future before it gets beyond our control.
A long silence followed, until Rocco grabbed the nearest woman to dance with, calling out. ` Let's party! `
Rocco had sent a telepathic message to his disc jockey Drone that livened up the party with Earth music from Rocco's time period. However, life is cruel and it was not all fun on planet Mayan.

Chapter Seventeen

A little later that night the locals, as expected, had not all accepted the indigenous species of planet Mayan. Who had been encouraged to leave their underground city and investigate life on the surface? After all, the Shadows could not be expected to remain below ground forever. Admittedly, they were shy, and very apprehensive to the surface living Mayans, and did not approach them. The language was a big barrier and local treatment brutal.
Rocco had mentioned that it reminded him of the Australian aborigines. How they had been persecuted and suffered.
It had happened before with other colonialists and no doubt would happen again; this time on Mayan. He was therefore unsurprised to learn that some unscrupulous bastards were feeding adventurous Shadows drink in exchange for services of the flesh while pumping them for information about the gold stored below in the city of Atlantis.

The Shadows had no resistance to the strong alcohol and it wasn't long before a young shadow had drunk a little too much alcohol. He had wanted to quietly enjoy the music at the party but envious eyes had seen his necklace of Gold with a fine ruby in the centre.
The local yobs, thinking he was incapable of resisting tried to remove it from his neck.
The young Shadow resisted and started to grow taller in order to defend himself. When someone produced a knife; there was a drunken struggle and the owner of the knife ended up dead.
A hue, and cry went up and the party ended as Elder took control by picking up the attackers, one in each hand by the throat.

He raised them kicking and screaming above the heads of the crowd and held them in that position until Rocco hastily arrived.

The crowd had gathered surrounding Elder and it was necessary for Rocco to fire his weapon into the air, to gain access.

On one side, friends of the inebriated shadow had gathered holding him back. On the opposite side baying for blood were the crowd, all pointing at the dead man who sat stiffly upright against a wall with his own knife sticking out of his throat.

Rocco and Tuwa marched the two Mayans out of the crowd and into custody. The boy was sent with Elder to sober up and get a knife wound stitched up.

Although the party resumed, everyone knew that things had changed forever!

The atmosphere and the music went flat reflecting their disappointment and broken hopes as the party crowd suddenly cleared leaving only the dedicated cleaners.

In the morning, the young Shadow was released to his friends and they were directed to return to the city of Atlantis.

The other two men were taken before a court where it was discovered they were not from Mayan, but visitors from the Conglomerate of planets who had gate crashed to specifically start trouble and cause a rift between the resident community and everyone else.

They had been instructed by the Conglomerate to increase disgruntlement so that the majority of the Mayan people would be acceptable to getting outside help and ultimately they hoped of acceptance of offered arms and manpower. They did not say what was expected in return.

Rocco immediately realised that the plan had very dangerous implications. they had obviously secretly planned, to convince the low cast Mayans, that they were their friends in trade and industry. They should reject the members of Freedom and the Shadows. Their objective was to obstruct, divide and conquer.
This would leave the Freedom Nation without support or friends and they; the Conglom, hoped that the people of Freedom would revert to the status of slaves and be once again controlled by them.
Rocco's headache increased with thoughts of interplanetary WAR!

The court, under advisement agreed to hold the two hostile interlopers for a while and round up any others before they got away to report what had happened. Rocco had already gathered some other members of visiting crafts and they were under guard.
The Star ships were alerted and a high level of security set, in case of an attack. This would give the Conglomerates a perfect excuse to start an all out war. He remembered how hostile they had acted when Tuwa had tried to cross-space to get to Freedom. He would never forget their aggression on Freedom when they wanted the trade rights.
At this point, Rocco relinquished all his interests to Tuwa who, as first Lord of the Mayan people, would be responsible for any action they may decide to take.
He and Appi returned to the Invistor Star with her parents, Ix-Chel and Captain Smiley.

 On the way over, Rocco had mentioned to Appi and Ix-Chel that he would be going down to the planet to find the cub, as soon as possible. He wanted Ix-Chel to accompany him as they would ask for help from the Sharpei.

Appi was not at all happy with this; it seemed to her to be more dangerous now than any other time. She asked that he should also take Elder as well, since he would be joining them later that evening.

Appi thought that with all this disquiet and aggression around the planets, they may get into serious trouble if the Conglomerate decided to attack before, Tuwa could organise a defence force.

The gathering on the Star, were in high spirits. It had been some time, since the whole family had actually sat down at the same table together to eat. Everyone seemed to be enjoying the meal with excited conversations about their exploratory trips and fantastic ancient finds on Mayan and the surrounding planets. The room filled with excited chatter that they did not initially notice, Nurse Chat-a-Lot arriving. She entered the room, with a strange pushchair that had been hastily constructed, by what the Drones conceived, as child transportation.

To their merit, the chair did hold the youngster, who was unnaturally restricted by leather straps that seemed too tight to be safe; some were placed in such a way, that they prevented movement. Its eyes seemed close to tears, with an un-natural look of panic.

The golden glow about its face had become flushed, combining all the colours into a deep Sunset blush, while franticly struggling to free itself as they drew nearer.

Following behind came the new Drone that had saved Rocco. He marched to the front and bowed as if just finishing a grand gala performance. But, no one seemed impressed.

The audience did not applaud; in fact, they remained embarrassingly dumb-folded into complete silence.

It was Rocco; that produced gasps from his friends, as he suddenly stood up, so fast, that his chair crashed behind him, making a terrible noise; drawing all their attentions, as he drew his knife. The tension in the room heightened, as he ran towards the child; which, crouched deeper into its chair, in a way that one would if trying to become smaller; in a desperate effort to disappear completely. But, the ties that held it were becoming tighter and one had slipped around its neck, squeezing its little head, restricting the blood flow, changing its face into a deep purple colour.

It was Rocco's speed of movement, which astonished the watchers as his knife flashed at lightning speed, entering and releasing, every single binding in a single stroke.

He leaned over and smiled at the child, who suddenly relaxed, watching him replace his weapon into its sheaf. Rocco knelt down to the same height as the pram, bringing them to equal eye level while sending a telepathic question to the child.

` My name is Rocco, what are you called?  ` The child turned its head away towards the Drone as though seeking a response; then it turned back and stared directly at Rocco, who repeated the same question again in his head, then with no response, he turned and spoke to the Drone. `Do you have a name or number? `   ` My designation is 478 Captain. `

Rocco continued, ` 478, does the child have a name? `   a short pause, ` It does not remember Captain. `

`478, is the child telepathic? `   `Yes Captain, in its original language of Areilium. `

` Oh, I see. Well 478, it is my wish that you transfer the Areilium language files that you have, to my device and also update my Nurse, Chat-a-Lot, so that we can speak with the child.  Please proceed to our communications centre; the chief Android will assist you.`   He then turned and spoke aloud to everyone at the table. ` Then perhaps we can find out what the child will eat? ` The Drone realising the importance of the question answered;   ` It is capable of eating anything Captain. `

`Thanks 478.  Let's try it on something simple. `

Rocco, quickly scribbled a simple recipe note, and sent one of the serving Drones down to the lounge kitchen.

Appi, curious as ever, could not resist, ` Husband, what did you order? ` He smiled in a teasing way, ` wait and see my little delight of loveliness. `

He turned away from her, knowing that she would be even more inquisitive as he cleared a space between himself and Captain Smiley. Rocco glanced at her face as he picked up the child and seated it at the table between Smiley and himself.

It wasn't long before a Drone appeared scurrying along the centre passage way, carrying a tall open container filled to the brim with ice. This it placed in front of them on the table. The child seemed to have settled now that its restraints had been remover. Its curiosity was plain to see as Rocco pulled out another smaller container, and removed the lid.

Then with a long spoon, scooped some of the contents and offered it to the child.

Everyone watched with some amusement as it sniffed the spoon and its contents, then it bravely allowed Rocco to place the melting sweetness into its mouth.

The whole company fell into silence; as the Childs eyes grew wider and wider. They watched as it gingerly tasted the sample; then suddenly, its taste buds kicked in as its mouth went   into a frenzy, causing its lips to   smack rapidly together, followed by a broad grin and a look of pure joy as Rocco handed over the spoon to allow it to help itself.

Appi looked across the table and nodded. ` My husband, I think it may be more girl than boy. ` She continued nodding in a knowing way.

He grinned, replying, ` I don't think any child could resist the pleasure of homemade Ice cream.
The atmosphere lifted suddenly changing as the room became much livelier with everyone talking at once; until another Drone arrived from the kitchen and served great helpings of Vanilla pod Ice cream to everyone.

At this point, Appi managed to set little April onto her lap, she made so much noise slurping but, not nearly as much as Ix-Chel and the new child; who began to look a little disappointed that its container was now empty. However, while no one was watching, Rocco made the ultimate sacrifice, by pushing half of his share across for the child to finish.
` I wonder, ` he pondered, ` If anyone can suggest a name for our new responsibility? `
 Appi and her father both thought this would be difficult, not knowing the gender! But, Appi's mother thought, it may prefer to have a name that doesn't match.
` Oh, there's no hurry, ` Smiley chipped in. ` The child may remember its own name in time. After all, I remembered my new name, only after a few days. ` Rocco roared with laughter as Smiley continued ` I only mention this because it has taken years to get used to my original name ` and gave an ironic smile at Rocco, ` Actually, I prefer the new name; but, how am I going to explain it to my family when they arrive from Moofee?? `

The rest of the day passed with humour followed with inevitable disappointment as the party began to end with the darkness of evening drawing the night ever closer. Suddenly, it was time to retire to their quarters, as friend Elder arrived, half expecting a great fuss to be made over him and his endurance with the trials and tribulations on the planet below.

Ix-Chel seemed pleased, that her compatriot was back, they had lots to tell, all about of the happenings on the planet below, and in return, he too chuckled at the proceedings of the day on the Invistor Star. However, he seemed just a little upset to learn that he missed the delights of the frozen Ice cream.

But, his mentor Captain Rocco, had arranged a special surprise for him, delivered by a Drone with decorum.

Early the following day, a small shuttle party transferred across to the Ja'Way and transported down directly to the village of the Sharpei on Shambala. Their arrival caused great surprise that culminated in a welcoming session of alcohol that Rocco had arranged as a bribe. He needed help for his select party with Ix-Chel, the new Drone 478, and at least four Sharpei.

He knew it would not be easy to convince the tribe to venture out of their comfort zone to accompany them to the area where Rocco had first encountered the tigers.

However, alcohol is a great stiffener of backbones and negotiations went well with Rocco accepted as a God and a promise of regular ambrosia now easily manufactured in great quantities; thanks to the Shadows endeavours and need.

The team left camp in high spirits, Rocco leading ahead of the group to lay his scent around the paths, hoping that the tiger cub would recognize and remember him.

In his mind, he hoped that despite the short time spent together, they had bonded and perhaps this may be enough to gain its trust.

Approaching the area Rocco sensed a strange eerie quietness as he exited the surrounding wooded perimeter. At first glance, it seemed that the clearing had been trampled flat.

His thoughts raced, about how, or what could have caused this devastation? He paused and waited for complete silence from the team and listened. Nothing could be heard, not a sound. Then someone sneezed and everyone jumped. Rocco glared at the culprit as they waited until there was total silence. He could see that the Sharpei had become very restless and decided that everyone should take cover within the line of trees while he slowly walked in alone.

Back on Mayan, all the delegates had returned to the meeting place after the previous days negotiations had failed. No one seemed to be able to accept the possibility of war. That concept had never been considered until now, that all the smaller planets had joined and become the New Coalition Alliance.
The N.C.Alliance, believed that the Conglomerate or old consortium were only interested in the slave planet of Freedom because of all its resources and a continuation of outside slave trade.
 But now, the Conglom, the name shortened by the locals for guttural convenience and amusement. (It implied a native sexual act, that made everyone smile and giggle as they repeated it like naughty children.)
However, despite the irritation, the Conglom had   been secretly keeping a round the clock vigil, with spies watching their every move as the N.C.A. Coalition slowly came together in friendship and trade; emerging as a strong force that caused some frustration and jealousy when the Conglom were not invited to join.

The position now was that the elected partners of Mayan and Freedom had shown strong leadership. This only slightly worried the Conglomerate, until the realisation of what was actually staring them in the face.

Six fully manned, armed, and working Battle Star ships.

It was a shock; and the Conglomerate, had unwittingly provoked it by their previous actions of aggressive behaviour; their enslavement of women and children from the planet Freedom. Their plans that had failed to take both planets using mercenary pirates.

They could neither see or believe that the N.C. Alliance was speedily growing in strength and wealth, turning the tables from reliance on the generosity of the surrounding planets.

In the past the Conglomerate had been the masters, they did not want to lose that status, but they had shown previously, their greed; and they still thought that they could get it all if they were to cause chaos and then divide the Alliance.

At the table meeting, Lord Tuwa had tried his best to persuade a few senior members, experienced in dealing with agitators and aggressive situations to accompany subordinates during selection of defensive positions on Mayan and Freedom.

Their previous experience was invaluable to the N.C.A. the committee had realised the importance of combining intelligence and communications between the planets as quickly as possible.

It had also been discussed (in Rocco's absence) that if the Invistor Star held a position around the orbit of Shambhala, they would have a triangular fix on all movements between the three planets. This of course was something they had learnt from Rocco's recent victory.

The Conglom outnumbered the Alliance in manpower by millions but, not in strength or arms, since their great find of

Atlantis. Nevertheless, a surprise attack especially on Freedom would be a catastrophe.

 Tuwa was in his element moving from the surface down to the City of Atlantis. He had chosen a large, main central position underground, to set up his headquarters.
He gathered around him all the leaders of the different factions, to plan and repulse an imminent attack, from the Conglomerate. The Shadows, now elected to be principle players, gave their voice (or screech perhaps would be more appropriate) to everything. As landlords of the City, it seemed only right to listen and share their opinions, especially when they grew in stature, which proved a useful way of getting attention, and winning an argument.
They were excellent fighters, and after some intelligent reasoning, they truly became informed and understood what might occur (especially to them) if war broke out.

The Shadows eventually came to agree that being allied and members of the N.C. Alliance, was far the best thing to do. But now; they had to be convinced that the surface dwellers should also join them in the City.
Lord Tuwa knew reluctantly that, he must designate someone to command and keep control of the city while he returned to deploy the Ja'Way. He secretly wished his friend Rocco could help him, he would be the best commander but, a second choice had to be made.
His thoughts were broken as Elder appeared with Lord Duvan and Lady Appisommati. The elderly statesman was after all a distinguished diplomat and leader during Moofee campaigns. Surely, with the help of friend Elder they could organize the defences. This, Tuwa thought ` was a stroke of genius. `

The committee assembled and voted. Lord Duvan was duly elected Governor of Atlantis and Elder reluctantly accepted the position of senior defence General, with the responsibility of deployment and operations.

Chapter Eighteen

On Shambhala, the rescue team was concerned about the clearing. Rocco thought it looked like the day after a large Circus had packed up all its equipment, tents, cages and left. Was circus the key? Could it have been a hunt for zoological purposes, like on Earth; or could they want to display these strange and different species?
 Rocco continued to look around and noted some tufts of hair and signs of dragging. Then he caught site of a type of matted material, a rope and his worst nightmare, a large bloodstain.
He contacted Appi on the Star, `what is it my love ` she whispered in a husky voice. He controlled his thoughts as he telepathed. ` I think the planet has been raided, all the animals have disappeared. It's like a giant vacuum has swallowed them all up. Even the birds have gone. `
Appi was silent with a long pause; Rocco was not prone to exaggeration. ` My husband, is it possible that they may have migrated to the furthest end of the valley? `
He was quick to reply and seemed angry, ` I have found rope and blood, and the whole area has been crushed with heavy equipment. No they have been taken !
She could feel the strain from his thoughts. ` We can make a search from here with heat sensing cameras. I will also check whether there are any ionised or R.A. particles trailing away from Shambhala.
He thanked her as he called the search party together, they would continue following the well-trodden route into the valley towards the mountains. The signs were easy to follow, and not difficult to imagine that a large construction had been dragged along from the open area. In a way, he thought it was possible that some of the animals were still alive.

Eventually they came to a place where the trail ended abruptly. It was a huge area with a distant horizon of mountains. `A spacecraft could easily land anywhere here, ` he thought, he ignored the huge range of mountains directly behind him that soared high and seemingly touched the clouds in the sky above.
He had not imagined such grand majesty on this planet with so many deserts, but they had not really explored the other expanses, or the area that lay within the dark side.

As the team marvelled at the beauty of the rock formation; Rocco rubbed the back of his neck, he felt something an energy force but ignored it. Then Ix-Chel spotted a face engraved high up on the facet of the apex.
She squealed and pointed for everyone to look up.
It was so far up that any normal person would have easily missed it.
At first they wondered how this had been achieved, it was impossible to climb the sheer granite face. The carving looked small from their position but Rocco mumbled something about, ` it is actually, very big.
What do you think is its purpose? Could it be connected to the Moon that we destroyed? ` Then he went on about distance. ` At this distance it's impossible to make a facial comparison , it would have to wait . ` He shivered as the hairs on his head seemed to stand up, like the spikes on a hedgehog, just before it rolled into a ball.
Rocco rubbed his neck; feeling again, something unusual, that made his whole body shiver.
 They were now very close to the mountain, and something like an electrical force of energy was tingling the nerves on the back of his neck. It was that feeling of an unnatural shiver, that everyone gets sometime during their life.

Rocco called it. ` Something walking on his grave, ` and the feeling got stronger as they moved nearer.

Ix-Chel had stopped moving altogether, she holding her head as in pain. The sharpie, were grovelling on the ground, also suffering as they struggled to crawl backwards away from that place. Strangely, Rocco and the Drone were not affected, but did not venture further forward.

He tried to contact the star but found that something was jamming his communications. So he and the Drone retreated and rejoined the team.

` We must inform the others in the command centre of the Star. This place has a strong security force shield which, seems to control everything except humans and Drones ? `

The Invistor Star had positioned itself directly above the valley of mysteries and by the time, Rocco and the team had retreated back to an area, well out of reach from the security zone where they needed to pause for breath and think. It was here during their recovery, that he received a message from Appi that they too, were experiencing difficulties.

They had strayed too close, to the valley while trying to contact him and some type of tractor beam, was trying to pull the Invistor Star directly towards the mountains.

Rocco's thoughts were racing, ` This is what happened to the other craft. He had to gain entry and stop the beam.

He raced ahead followed more sedately by the Drone 478.

The interference returned, but this time they did not stop until they reached the base of the mountain where Rocco and the Drone evaporated, completely disappearing.

Something had grabbed and teleported them into the mountain which as they recovered from the shock revealed a vast complex of modern machinery with cages of dead animals and mixed Sharpei.

First things first thought Rocco, and shouted `478; find the tractor beam and the security power supply, and TURN THEM OFF !! `
It was hopeless. How were they going to find anything in this massive warren? The time was ticking and it had to be done now.
Rocco shocked and high on adrenalin knew he had to be quick otherwise the Star would have the same fate as the other craft. He drew his pistol and fired at everything resembling a power source or generator; causing explosions that multiplied in sequence, generating a destructive cycle all around as he ran in every direction. Rocco was frantic and close to raging madness, as he ran from area to area shooting and destroying, wondering where Drone 478 had disappeared to.

Then everything became radiated in brilliant white light before a great roar followed with a blinding cloud of swirling dust that surrounded him.
It was a massive explosion that knocked him to the floor; giving the impression that a great portal had opened up around him.
He lay helplessly stretched out in the centre of the calm area of a tornado, which did not move. Stunned, unable to do or move anything, he watched as the dust particles slowly began to change shape.

 He imagined that he could see the outline of people gliding toward him, somehow they were hovering above the floor level, slowly advancing as the dust and smoke gave way to their forward movements. Each apparition appeared to be dressed in a shimmering white shroud and he marvelled at how each swayed in rhythm to the glittering movements of their attire. They were encapsulated in an aura of colour, reflecting a life source of spiritual beings that encircled and locked as each member moved into the circle surrounding him. Making an unbreakable bound; around the perimeter of the circle, enclosing him safely, within.